Halloween Hijinks
Anniversary Edition

A Zoe Donovan Mystery
With Additional Recipes

And Special Short Story
Zoe's Treasure Hunt

by

Kathi Daley

D0112885

Version 1.0

Copyright © 2014 by Katherine Daley

This book is dedicated to my very patient friend Paul Dinas. Paul is a talented editor and writing coach who took a dreamer and gave me the tools I would need to reach my goals. Not only did Paul help me to develop my potential as a writer, but he is the one who suggested I write cozies in the first place. So thank you Paul. XOXOX

Also a special thank you to the very talented Jessica Fischer, who reworked the cover for this special edition. Jess, I couldn't have done it without you.

And a thank you as well to readers Darcy Weber and Diane Fleming for helping with the copy edit of the old text. I also want to thank my editor Randy Ladenheim-Gil for the editing of the new text.

And of course thank you to Christy, Carrie, Brennen, Cristin, and Danny for sharing and providing input.

And last but not definitely not least, I want to thank my super-husband Ken for allowing me time to write by taking care of everything else.

Table of contents

Books by Kathi Daley

Paradise Lake Series:
Pumpkins in Paradise
Snowmen in Paradise
Bikinis in Paradise
Christmas in Paradise – September 2014
Puppies in Paradise – February 2015

Zoe Donovan Mysteries:
Halloween Hijinks
The Trouble With Turkeys
Christmas Crazy
Cupid's Curse
Big Bunny Bump-off
Beach Blanket Barbie
Maui Divas
Haunted Hamlet – August 2014
Turkeys, Tuxes, and Tabbies – October 2014
Christmas Cozy – November 2014
Alaskan Alliance – December 2014

Road to Christmas Romance:
Road to Christmas Past

Halloween Hijinks

Chapter 1

It was the week before Halloween and the alpine town of Ashton Falls was decorated festively for the annual Haunted Hamlet: a four-day event comprised of a haunted barn, spooky maze, zombie run, kiddie carnival, and pumpkin patch. Known as the event capital of the Timberland Mountains, Ashton Falls is a quaint village, nestled on the shore of a large deepwater lake, surrounded by hundreds of miles of thick evergreen forest.

Like many small towns across the country, Ashton Falls is a village with a big heart but a tiny local budget. While our forefathers tended toward rugged isolation, the younger generation has discovered that the answer to funding luxuries such as a free public library, volunteer fire department, afterschool sports and activities and, my personal favorite, wild and domestic animal control and rehabilitation, is a steady inflow of tourist dollars from the larger cities in the valley below. After much consideration, the town council decided that the best way to accomplish the aforementioned transfer of funds was the frequent hosting of an array of celebrations and events. As a result of this constant state of preparation and implementation, the Ashton Falls Events Committee, of which I am a member, was formed.

My name is Zoe Donovan. I'm a third-generation Ashtonite (our unofficial name for the citizens of our little community). The by-product of my wealthy mother's single act of teenage rebellion, and my locally beloved but financially lacking, blue-collar father's tender act of love, I've overcome my scandalous entry into the world and carved out a satisfying and peaceful existence. While some of the crustier old geezers in town would say I have a tendency toward the absurd, I like to think that I'm actually a normal and well-rounded twenty-four-year-old with a few adorable quirks that make me, me.

According to my Facebook page, which I share with Charlie, my half terrier/ half mystery dog, we're in a relationship with our two cats, a huge orange tabby named Marlow (after detective Phillip Marlow) and a petite black beauty named Spade (named for Sam Spade and not the playing card suit.) We are avid joggers and mystery buffs who work for the Ashton Falls branch of the Timberland County Animal Shelter. When we aren't rescuing animals and placing them in homes around the community, I volunteer at the senior center, where I horn in on their book club, and Charlie volunteers at the hospital, where he's a therapy dog. I like to wakeboard in the summer and snowboard in the winter, while Charlie prefers chasing a Frisbee on the beach or hiking the miles of unmarred forest around the lake. We both like to relax by curling up in front of the fire with a good book in the converted boathouse we call home.

I suppose I should mention that, although I tend to be verbally creative and a bit long-winded, I'm not a physically impressive individual. In fact, at five foot two (okay, five foot nothing) and just under a hundred pounds, I'm considered by most to be both vertically challenged and physically derisory. I inherited my dad's stick-thin frame, speckling of freckles, and thick curly hair, a deep chestnut brown that most days is a wild mess that I braid or just pull back with a large clip. I've been told I have nice eyes, sort of an intense yet unusual piercing blue, and I did manage to inherit my mother's long, thick lashes and wide, full-lipped smile.

I guess the only other thing you should know is that, while I'm somewhat high-strung in general, I tend to go more than a little nuts if the equilibrium in my most important relationships is disturbed in any way. I'm not sure where my neurotic need to maintain homogeneity originated, but I suspect it had something to do with my mom's desertion when I was just a baby.

My story begins on a sunny Tuesday in October. Although the temperature was unseasonably warm and the air delightfully calm, I knew, intuitively, that a storm was brewing. The storm wouldn't be a traditional sort, embodying rain and lightning-streaked skies but a different type, born of the tangled threads of iniquitous secrets and ravaged lives.

Charlie and I were on our way to the regular Tuesday morning breakfast meeting of the Ashton Falls Events Committee when we noticed two of the members of the Ashton Falls Bulldogs (rugged, blue-collar-raised mountain boys with a tendency toward mischief) hanging a mannequin in the town square dressed in a jersey they stole —I later found out— from the locker room of their arch rivals, the Bryton Lake Beavers (think upper-class preppy in a tries-too-hard, middle-class sort of way). This year, for some maniacal reason, the biggest football game of the decade was scheduled the same weekend as the annual Haunted Hamlet, one of the town's biggest fund-raisers of the year. While the pregame psych-out is a time-honored tradition in our little corner of the world, this year, with the matchup of historical rivals, both undefeated, the pranks, it seemed, had been steadily escalating for days.

I made a left-hand turn in front of Trish's Treasures—think touristy-type establishment selling a variety of objects with ASHTON FALLS branded on the front—when I noticed my best friend, Levi Denton, talking to the boys in question. Levi is the coach at the local high school. An athletic jack-of-all-trades, he coaches football in the fall, basketball in the winter, and baseball in the spring. Levi and I, along with the other member of our triad, Ellie Davis, have been best friends since kindergarten, when everyone sat at round tables of three, alphabetically by last name.

"Trouble?" I asked as Levi approached the parking lot where I had pulled in next to his 4Runner. Although he looked tired, Levi is a handsome man: six foot two, thick brown hair, sun-kissed skin from the hours he spends outdoors, and muscles that prove he walks his talk and pays a visit to the gym almost every day.

"Warren Trent was in an accident last night." Levi referred to his star running back. "He's going to be okay, but he broke his leg in three places, so it looks like he'll be out for the season."

"What happened?"

"Some idiot in a truck swerved toward him while he was riding his bike home from practice. Warren tried to avoid a collision and ended up in the drainage ditch that runs along the highway. The moron in the truck didn't even stop to see if he was okay."

"You don't think…" The biggest game of the season and the teams' star running back is involved in an accident?

"I don't know. I hope not. But maybe." Levi sighed. I frowned as I noticed the worry lines around his dark green eyes making him look much older than his twenty-four years. "The guys on the team think it might be payback for the skunk incident."

"Skunk incident?"

"Monday, after the guys saw the field, one of the guys on the team caught a skunk and locked it in Kirby Wall's gym locker after stealing his jersey. I guess it completely destroyed Kirby's gear, as well as stinking up the whole locker room." I knew that Kirby was the starting quarterback for the Beavers, and one of the most obstreperous idiots in the whole county. Kirby had been trash-talking the Bulldogs for months. I really wasn't surprised that the guys had chosen Kirby as their victim, but I wasn't thrilled they used an innocent skunk as their weapon.

"Field?" The entirety of what Levi had just said finally hit home. While the dance to gain one-upmanship was, as I said, a time-honored tradition, it looked like the familiar waltz was taking an early toll on the normally energetic and enthusiastic coach.

"The guys from Bryton Lake painted a giant beaver giving the one-finger salute over the top of the Bulldog in the center of the field." Levi sighed again. "Principal Lamé isn't happy about any of this and is threatening the suspension of any and all students involved if the pranks continue."

I knew that Principal Joe Lamé—pronounced La-mae with an exaggerated accent—was new to Ashton Falls this year, a transplant from a school in the valley who apparently woke up one day and decided to embrace the mountain way of life. While I understand the desire one might have to live in this beautiful place I call home, I'm afraid the yuppie simply doesn't get our small town ways. The difference in perspective has resulted in a sort of low, humming tension, between the man and his staff and students.

"I've tried taking to the boys," Levi continued, "but honestly, I don't think my warnings of 'severe consequences' for random acts of vandalism are really sinking in. If you want my opinion, I think the guys are intentionally trying to raise lamebrain's blood pressure."

"So who exactly started the whole thing?" I tucked a stray lock of hair behind my ear as I tried to work out the sequence of events in my mind.

"I think I may have."

"You?" I was surprised. Levi is an easygoing sort of guy who normally isn't inclined toward bellicose acts of unsportsmanlike conduct.

"Not intentionally," Levi defended himself. "Last Friday I was a guest on that morning show, *Wake Up Timberland*, and I made a sarcastic remark about the Beavers new wide receiver, Samantha Collins." I knew that Samantha was the first female in the county to play high school ball after her parents had challenged her right to do so in court and won.

"I thought I was being funny, but I guess Coach Griswold didn't see it that way. Later that morning he called my office and left me a scathing phone message," Levi continued.

Coach Griswold had spoken out quite passionately during the court hearing in opposition to Samantha's inclusion on the team. I had to admit that

I was impressed that he was sticking up for Samantha in spite of the fact he'd been quite vocal in his campaign to have her removed from the team.

"I realized that my joke, while not intended to be malicious, was actually mean-spirited and uncalled for," Levi continued. "I called Griswold and apologized. I thought that was the end of it until we showed up at practice on Saturday and saw a giant beaver where our bulldog used to be."

"So the kids on your team put a skunk in Kirby's locker and stole his jersey as payback for the graffiti," I guessed.

"Sounds about right."

"And you think Warren was run off the road as a return of the symbolic volley?"

"Personally I can't imagine that anyone would do such a thing, but Warren remembers the vehicle that swerved into him was a white truck, and Coach Griswold drives a white truck. Everyone knows Griswold is a narcissist who will do anything to win."

I wrapped my arm around Levi's waist and laid my cheek against his chest. "I'm sorry. Anything I can do?" Levi isn't just a babe; he's sweet and thoughtful and considerate as well. There are those in town, including my father, who don't understand why we haven't moved our relationship to a more intimate level. The thing is, I love Levi way too much to risk screwing up what we have with a messy romantic encounter. Besides, with Ellie in the mix, a three-way friendship is an easier dynamic than a couple and a third wheel.

"No, but thanks for asking." He kissed the top of my head. "How about you? Any luck finding zombies for the run?"

"Afraid not," I said. "If there's anyone who could use a zombie apocalypse right about now it would be me. I'm not sure what I'll do if I can't scare up some willing brain eaters."

This year I'm in charge of the annual zombie run. For those of you who are unfamiliar with this awesome event, it's sort of like a regular 5K fun run, except you're chased by hungry, merciless zombies who want to eat your brain. You're given flags at the beginning of the race that the zombies want to steal. If you lose all your flags, you're dead. Only the most cunning and agile can make it out alive. Normally the guys from the football team are happy to tap into their inner zombie and chase willing participants through Black Bear Woods, but this year, with the big game scheduled for the same weekend as the run, most are too preoccupied to sign up.

"I'll talk to the guys and see if I can get a few volunteers," Levi offered.

"Thanks. I'd really appreciate that."

"How many do you still need?"

I thought about it. So far the only walking dead I'd managed to round up were a few of the guys from the senior center, and half of them would be chasing runners using walkers and oxygen tanks. "As many as I can get," I answered.

"Okay, I'll see what I can do. I need to get back to the school, so I'll be a few minutes late to the committee meeting. Can you order me a mountain man special and tell the others I'll be along shortly?"

After Levi walked away I turned to Charlie, who had been waiting patiently on the passenger seat. "I think it's going to be a tough week for everyone. What do you say we invite Levi and Ellie to a BBQ at the house so that everyone can forget the insanity that has befallen our little town for a few hours?"

Charlie barked in response. Second only to me, I think Levi is Charlie's favorite person. Not only does Levi always greet him with a kind word and a vigorous scratch on the belly, but my friend, on more than one occasion, has slipped him a piece of his steak or burger when he thinks I'm not looking.

After Levi got into his vehicle and drove away, Charlie and I carefully maneuvered the mammoth we drive out of the tightly spaced parking lot. I drive a truck: a big one. A four-wheel drive, heavy-duty, extra-cab, lift-kit enhanced, long- bed monster. Although it takes a leap worthy of a pole-vaulter for me to enter the beast, and parking is a problem more often than not, I find its size necessary given the fact that I live and work in an environment in which half of the miles I log each year are spent plowing through waist-deep snow or jolting along rutted dirt roads. A big, heavy truck is essential. The truck is black with tinted windows and a raised, camper-type shell built specifically to safely store animal crates of different sizes, which, thanks to my dad, are secured to the bed of the vehicle to avoid sliding.

I carefully executed a twenty-point turn and pulled out of the parking lot and onto Main Street, which was decked out for the upcoming weekend celebrations. The school colors for my alma mater are black and gold, chosen by my forefathers to represent the inky blackness of the deep underground mines our ancestors worked and the ever-elusive gold few were lucky enough to find. Luckily, this color scheme works equally well for the Haunted Hamlet, necessitating only one set of decorations for both events.

I suppose this is a good place to mention that the original name for the mining camp where Ashton Falls now sits was Devil's Den. Not a cozy name, to be sure, but probably a bit more accurate than the somewhat pretentious Ashton Falls, a name given to the town by Ashton Montgomery, a multimillionaire and my great-grandfather on my mother's side. Ashton bought the land where the village now stands and built the town as sort of a touristy tribute to himself (no vanity there). At one time all the land in the mountain basin where Ashton Falls is located was owned by the Montgomery's, but, unlike Ashton, his three sons weren't thrilled with the mountain way of life and moved from the area as soon as they were old enough to hitch their horses to wagons heading west. (Actually, they went away to college, never to return to the isolated mountain town, but I thought the wagon-heading-west analogy was a bit more poetic.)

After Ashton died, his sons, Bryce, Jamison, and Preston—my grandfather— divided the land and began selling it off, keeping in the family only a few prime pieces of property, such as the isolated bay where my converted boathouse sits. Of the three sons, my grandfather Preston is the only one who continued to visit Ashton Falls after his father's death. Every summer he'd bring his wife, three sons, and daughter —my mother—to the mansion he built overlooking the lake for two months of what he laughingly labeled "rugged mountain living." That, by the way, is how my mother met my father and yours truly was conceived, but that is a story for another day.

Anyway, as I mentioned what seems an eon ago, the town of Ashton Falls is all decked out in the school colors of black and gold. The main street of our little town is built on the lakeshore, so as you drive through town from east to west, the lake, beach, and landscaped park area is on your left and the row of mom-and-pop shops and restaurants that gives Ashton Falls its quaint alpine charm is on the right. On both sides of the road is a walkway that's adorned with old-fashioned lampposts donated by my mother's family for the town's fiftieth-anniversary celebration. At first I thought the lights—white wrought- iron with fancy, lantern-shaped lights, three to a post—a bit ostentatious for our rugged little town, but as time has passed, these beacons, currently decorated with black and gold ribbons, have grown on me.

If there's one thing you can say for our little town, it's that we know how to improvise. Not only are most storefronts along the two-mile main drag decorated for the upcoming Haunted Hamlet, but they've adapted their displays in support of team pride for the upcoming football game as well. The barber shop decorated its doorway with black and gold twinkle lights, the bakery has a giant cake featuring zombies playing football in its front window, and the sporting goods store has a football-themed Halloween display complete with various life-size monsters dressed in retired jerseys from several generations of Ashton Falls Bulldogs.

I waved to Lilly Evans as I pulled up in front of Rosie's Cafe. Lilly, a seventy- two-year-old mother of four and grandmother of twelve, was perched precariously on a ladder in front of Second Hand

Suzie's, hanging a hand-painted sign that said BULLISH ON BULLDOGS.

"'Morning, Lilly," I said.

"'Mornin', Zoe. You, too, Charlie." Charlie trotted over to the ladder and sat down to wait for Lilly, dressed for fall in a burnt-orange sweater and a pair of khaki slacks, to climb down. "Guess you heard that Bears and Beavers was hit last night. That makes four robberies in the past two weeks."

"Same MO?" I wondered. Bears and Beavers is a touristy-type shop featuring souvenirs having to do with—you guessed it—bears and beavers. While many of the items are quite charming, I can't imagine what the store might stock that would interest a burglar. In the previous three cases, the thief snuck in, stole what seemed to be select yet inexpensive items, and then left, locking the door on the way out. It almost seemed like our late-night bandit was participating in some sort of elaborate scavenger hunt.

"Looks like."

"You'd think the sheriff would have caught the guy by now," I commented.

"You'd think, but we *are* talking about Sheriff Salinger." Lilly rolled her eyes.

The sheriff of Ashton Falls is really more of a reject from the county office in Bryton Lake. His father was a cop, as was his grandfather, so simply firing him from the force wasn't really an option. When the mayor of Bryton Lake decided that the socially awkward young recruit wasn't sophisticated enough for their uppity little town, Salinger was transferred to the satellite office in Ashton Falls. He'd been serving our town for almost twenty years, yet on most days of the week, he lets it be known to anyone who will listen that his time in our "hick" community is nothing more than a stepping stone to bigger things ahead.

"By the way, did Victoria call you about that raccoon in her attic?" Lilly added.

"Yeah. I'll head over and pick it up after the meeting." While my primary job—at least according to the county—is to monitor and control the domestic dog and cat population, it's well known in the area that if you're having a problem of the wild animal kind, my partner Jeremy and I are the ones to call.

"Heard you're gonna release that cub you picked up out behind my place last spring."

"We are," I answered as Lilly climbed down the ladder. "He's old enough to make it on his own. We've picked out a nice den for him to hibernate in over the winter. Jeremy is going to get him settled in over the next few weeks. We've tagged him so we can keep an eye on him, but I think he's going to be fine."

"That's good. I worried about the little guy after I heard his mama got hit by a car on the highway. Old girl lived in the forest behind my place for a good five years. Miss seein' her eatin' from my berry bush. Used to be a lot more wildlife in this area. Now most days it's just me and Kuba."

"I meant to ask how Kuba was doing." I referred to her fourteen-year-old lab, which had been injured in an altercation with a mountain lion.

"Okay, considering. I had Trevor put a fence around the yard a few weeks ago. Kuba is as curious as she ever was, but she's getting too old to defend herself, so I've decided I need to keep her closer to home. Don't know if you heard that Trevor broke up with that girl from the valley last month."

"Yeah, I heard." Lilly is a sweetheart, but she is forever trying to fix me up with her grandson, even though Trevor and I have both made it perfectly clear that neither of us is interested in anything more than a friendship.

"Trevor is a good boy," Lilly tried. "He'll make someone a damn good husband."

"I'm sure he will," I agreed. I like Trevor and he will, I am certain, one day make someone a wonderful husband, but the truth of the matter is, we just don't click. "I guess I should head in. I don't want to be late for the meeting." Actually, I was early, but I knew if I didn't make my escape, Lilly would have Trevor and me engaged faster than you can say "Grandma's biological clock."

"Hold on, I have a cookie for Charlie." Lilly fished a dog biscuit out of her pocket. "Are you going to the haunted barn?" she asked as she handed the treat to Charlie.

"I plan to."

"Got a date?"

"I do," I confirmed. My "date" was Ellie, but Lilly didn't need to know that.

"Oh." Lilly sighed. "That's too bad. I've been trying to talk Trev into going, but he isn't keen on goin' alone."

"Trevor is a handsome guy. I'm sure he can find a date if he really wants to go. Thanks for the cookie," I added on Charlie's behalf as I turned and made my escape through the front door of Rosie's.

Chapter 2

Rosie's is the quintessential alpine cafe perched snuggly on the shoreline of Ashton Lake; it's surrounded by tall pines and quaking aspens that turn a brilliant yellow every autumn. The large log cabin was originally built in the 1960s by a man named Lester Newton. Not a traditional mountain man name, I'll grant you, but a traditional mountain man all the same. Lester came to Ashton Falls in the mid-1950s, before the area had been settled as a year-round destination. He built the cafe originally as a house, but as the years passed and the town of Ashton Falls grew up around the once-isolated cabin, Lester decided to move his residence to a more private location and turned the old homestead into the best cafe this side of...well, this side of anywhere.

Named after Lester's wife, Rosie's is the type of place where friends are treated like family and family are considered to be friends. On any given day, between the hours of six a.m. and two p.m., locals and visitors alike gather at Rosie's to share a meal and catch up on the latest news. Built on the north shore of the lake, Rosie's takes full advantage of the view with a wall of large windows nestled between knotty pine logs that make up the frame of the rugged, hand-milled cabin.

The cafe is decorated with an eclectic assortment of skis, sleds, snowshoes, fishing poles, climbing ropes, and other antiques that define the area, while tables, both large and small, are arranged within the open and airy room around a huge floor-to-ceiling fireplace.

"Go on back." my best friend, Ellie Davis, directed. "I just want to grab some of mom's pumpkin muffins for the meeting."

"Better bring extra. I love your mom's muffins and the pumpkin are my favorite." I waved to Rosie; Ellie's fifty-four year old mother and café owner whose real name is Lorraine but changed it to Rosie when she bought the café. When I was young, Rosie sort of adopted me. Don't get me wrong: my dad is and was a fantastic parent, but sometimes a girl needs a mom. My relationship with my own mother is sort of an obligatory one; she shows up every now and then for some "quality" mother-and-daughter bonding, and I pretend to give a damn that she even wants to be a part of my life. And while I love my mother in my own way—I mean, she *is* my mom—it has always been Rosie who I turn to when I need a mother's warm hug, caring ear, wise word, and welcoming smile.

I continued through the cafe and down the stairs leading to the banquet room, where we hold our regular meeting. I poured myself a cup of coffee from the sideboard, settled Charlie at my feet, and sat down at the still empty table. Due to health regulations, dogs usually aren't allowed inside the dining area, but being well-known as a therapy dog, Charlie has always been given a pass.

I know there are people in the community who don't really get my relationship with Charlie. Most don't understand why I treat him more like a person than a dog. And while I have a soft spot in my heart for all of God's creatures, I have a special love for

Charlie, with whom I share a special bond. Charlie came into the world as the embarrassing product of Lorie Wilson's champion Tibetan terrier, Tiara Jane, and a mystery date who shall forever remain unnamed. After Charlie was born, the only pup in that unfortunate litter, Lorie wanted nothing to do with him, so Charlie came to live with me when he was only a few hours old. During those first few weeks when I struggled to keep him alive and healthy, we bonded in a way that even I can't entirely explain.

"Hey, squirt." My arch nemesis, Zak Zimmerman, walked into the room and sat down beside me.

"What are you doing here?" I wasn't pleased at the unexpected arrival of our local computer genius and all-around pain in my ass.

"I ran into Levi at The Pub last night and he encouraged me to join your little group."

"Terrific," I groaned.

My disdain for Zak is one of long-standing, with historical roots planted as far back as the seventh grade. In retrospect, I guess the incident, which led to months of uncontrolled sobbing and persistent feelings of self-loathing on my part, wasn't entirely his fault. He beat me quite soundly in the mathathon, for which I'd been studying relentlessly for almost three months. Yes, I was humiliated when I discovered that he'd only just found out about the event the previous day, indicating that he had spent virtually no time wallowing, as I had, in academic angst. Yes, I'd invited my maternal grandparents, a scary couple I'd met only a handful of times yet still inexplicably wanted to please, and yes, miracle of miracles, this untouchable couple, who valued achievement above all else, actually agreed to come to this lowly competition after being assured by my overachieving mother that I was the brightest student in the class and would win by a landslide.

"Perhaps your time would be better spent on one of the other town committees," I suggested. "I hear they always need volunteers for litter control."

"Is that your way of saying you missed me?"

It had been over a year since Zak had been home. While I spent most of my high school years studying my brains out in an attempt to beat Zak at—well, pretty much anything—he was busy building a software company in his garage. Seven days after his twenty-first birthday, he sold the enterprise to Microsoft for tens of millions of dollars, and he's been dividing his time between Ashton Falls and the rest of the world ever since.

"About as much as I miss the stomach flu I got last winter," I shot back. Truth be told, I did sort of miss the gadfly, but I'd sooner spend the winter cleaning the grease pit at the Burger Barn than admit it.

Zak just smiled and winked. A familiar gesture he knows I hate. The thing about Zak is that he knows I loathe him and yet he goes out of his way to be sugar and spice and everything nauseating. It drives me totally insane, which, I have decided, has been his plan all along. Deciding not to fall victim to the egghead's little mind games, I changed the subject to the one thing we both actually agree on: our love for our four-legged best friends.

"How's Lambda?" I asked, referring to the shelter dog Zak adopted four years ago.

"He's good. He developed a bit of arthritis in his bum leg, but I got some medication and he seems to be doing better. I've been working up his endurance by walking him along the lakeshore since we've been home."

"That's a good idea, but don't overdo it," I warned. "Other than the leg everything seems to be okay?"

"Yeah, he seems happy. He's glad to be home. I think he missed you."

"Yeah, I missed him, too," I said and meant it. Lambda, a chocolate lab, had been involved in a run-in with a black bear. Near death when I found him, I brought him to the shelter and nursed him back to health with the help of my assistant, Jeremy Fisher, and our volunteer shelter veterinarian, Scott Walden. Lambda was a young dog at the time of the attack and healed quickly, but his altercation left him with some permanent disabilities, and I worried about his ability to age gracefully.

"I'll bring him by the shelter sometime this week," Zak volunteered. "I know he'd love to see you."

"That would be nice. I'm sure Scott and Jeremy would love to see him, too."

I was spared the need to make further chitchat by the arrival of Ellie and my dad, both of whom greeted Zak with warm hugs and heartfelt wishes. Sometimes I feel awash in a sea of Zak lovers. No one really gets why the guy irritates me so much, and most think my disdain for his very existence is petty and mean-spirited. Sometimes even I don't understand why the guy pushes my buttons the way no one else can. Sure, I came in second to his first in every science fair, math Olympics, and spelling bee I entered from the day I first laid eyes on him in the seventh grade to the day we both graduated in the twelfth. But that was years ago, and you'd think I'd be over it by now. Could it be that everyone is right and I really am being spiteful?

I was saved the agony of further self-analysis by the arrival of the other members of the Ashton Falls Events Committee. I receive a good 30 percent of my budget from fund-raising activities, so I have a good reason to be involved. Other committee members include Levi, whose after-school sports program is largely supported through the high school booster club and local fund-raising events; Ellie, who runs an after-school dance program; Hazel Hampton, our local librarian, who like me, depends on a myriad of income sources; Tawny Upton, who owns and runs the Over the Rainbow preschool; Gilda Reynolds, who owns Bears and Beavers and runs a local theater arts program; Frank Valdez, who owns Outback Hunting and Fishing and runs a summer camp for teens; my dad, Hank Donovan, who owns Donovan's, a sort of general store, and represents the volunteer firefighters; and our leader and Ashton Falls town representative Willa Walton.

The money earned from fund-raising activities is funneled through the town's discretionary account. In theory, the money can be used in any way the town sees fit, but custom dictates that the funds generally are funneled back to the programs whose representatives earned the money in the first place. Willa's job as a representative of the town is to act as a mediator between the committee and the town council, which has final approval of all budgetary decisions. The Haunted Hamlet is one of our biggest-netting events and the members of the committee take their planning seriously.

"Does anyone have anything to add to the minutes of the last meeting?" Willa began once we had all given Rosie our breakfast orders. Willa is a good match for the job she performs. Controlled and professional in both dress and behavior, she runs a tight ship and can be counted on to cross all the t's and dot all the i's. Sometimes this makes for unbearably long meetings as she carefully and methodically makes her way through every step of the process, but having accurate records has saved more than one friendship over the years.

"The minutes state that forty percent of the kids at the preschool attended with scholarships provided by this group," Tawny, a thirty-two-year-old single mother of two, began. "I updated my spreadsheet and realized that we were up to forty-six percent after this year's enrollment was completed. With the current economic trend, I expect the percentage of parents requiring full or partial scholarships to increase by as much as ten percent next semester. Therefore I'd like to adjust the dollar amount of my funding request, if it's not too late."

"Any objections?" Willa asked, although I noticed a furrowing of the neatly maintained brows framing her medium brown eyes. She ran a hand impatiently through her short hair as first Hazel and then my dad objected, and the debate commenced.

I listened and Willa took notes as the group discussed the impact Tawny's request would have on the other projects the committee had agreed to fund. It was the same every year. Donations were shrinking at the same time needs were increasing. Holding a carnival, festival, or some other fund-raising event every few weeks was taking its toll on all of us, and as of late, the money we raised simply wasn't enough. We needed another strategy, and fast.

I watched as faces around the table changed from friendly to, in some cases, hostile, as representatives from each group fought to protect its territory. Were the needs of the preschoolers really more important than a free public library or food for the hungry? And if we cut the volunteer firefighters, how many homes and businesses would be left unprotected? The arguments were the same and therefore predictable, so I averted my attention to Levi, who snuck in during the debate and sat down across from me. He looked troubled and tired and appeared to be paying no more attention to the debate than me.

My heart ached for him. Lamé would be on him to put a stop to the pregame hazing, and I knew the guys weren't going to give up the battle if the ball ended up in their proverbial court. I gave him "the look," sort of a shorthand we'd developed over the years to communicate during the endless meetings we both attended.

My phone vibrated as he texted me from under the table. I don't know how he does that. If I didn't look at what I was texting, I'd end up with gibberish, but Levi is quite proficient at the art. I looked down at my phone. The message read: JSY'S DSTRY'D. B R UP 4 PB.

I knew from reading Levi's shorthand over the years that the game-day jerseys somehow had been destroyed and the Ashton Falls Bulldogs were on a rampage. I glanced at Zak, who was totally invading my space by reading my very private and personal text over my shoulder. He frowned, brows that matched the sun-bleached blond of his shoulder-length hair pursed in concern. His blue eyes met mine as we shared an unspoken message. Then I noticed Ellie was watching our silent exchange. I sent her a quick text, she nodded, and I looked at Zak, who shot a text to Levi just seconds before Willa asked Hazel to go over the official schedule for the weekend.

"The Haunted Hamlet opens on Wednesday with the haunted barn and spooky maze," Hazel began as Zak shifted his tall frame beside me. While I'm a bit on the petite side, Zak is a monster. We're talking Frankenstein freakishly tall. Given the fact that both of Zak's parents are on the diminutive side, it has long been speculated that Zak's father isn't really Zak's father at all. According to town gossip, Zak's mother had been keeping company with a retired basketball player from out west while Zak's father was overseas on business. Zak was born only eight months after his father's return. The family moved away until Zak was in the seventh grade, when his mother moved back to Ashton Falls with a new man who, it's rumored, is actually the younger brother of Zak's real dad. Confusing? You bet. And probably complete fiction.

"Both events will be open daily through Saturday, as will the pumpkin patch, the hay rides, and the haunted marathon at the theater," Hazel continued. "Due to the fact that the biggest game of the decade happened to fall on the same weekend as the Haunted Hamlet, the high school is sponsoring a special Halloween-themed pep rally on Friday morning. The game is Friday evening," Hazel added. "We're asking everyone to wear costumes to both the pep rally and the game."

Levi frowned. I knew he was less than thrilled with the fact that the biggest game of his career was being turned into a freakish spectacle, with zombies on the sideline, but I also knew he'd be too polite to say anything.

"On Saturday," Hazel continued, "we start off with the annual zombie run at eight. There will be a chili cook-off in the park and a jack-o'-lantern stroll Saturday evening. Because Halloween is on Saturday this year, the town council voted to hand out candy along Main Street so the kids could trick-or-treat while their parents enjoy the jack-o'-lantern display."

"And the pumpkin-carving contest?" Tawny asked.

"Saturday afternoon in the park," Hazel answered. "The only event that will be held on Sunday is the community picnic. Ellie is in charge of the picnic, so I'll turn the floor over to her."

Ellie went through the list of duties that had been assigned to everyone at the last meeting and requested updates. Levi was in charge of organizing a flag football game and my dad was procuring volunteers to man the BBQs, while Hazel was handling the potluck. My contribution to the weekend, in addition to helping man the pet adoption booth at the community picnic and providing zombies for the zombie run, is to organize carnival games for the kids. I have no children myself, and although I have little idea what types of games would entertain the minimally skilled youth of our town, my plan is simply to replicate the offerings that have been presented in the past.

I made a mental note to add a stop during my rounds today to ask Ernie Young, the not-so-young owner of the local market, if he'd be willing to donate balloons for the dart toss and candy for the fishing booth. Personally, I don't really get why tossing a string attached to a pole over a blanket-covered line is considered by the five-and-under crowd to be a boatload of fun, but based on last year's data, of which I have familiarized myself in the interest of boatloads of quarters, the fishing booth brought in more donations than any other booth, so I went ahead and included it in this year's selection.

I watched Levi as he got up to answer a phone call. This week was going to be hard on him. It was only Tuesday and the game wasn't until Friday. He was going to have a tough time keeping the guys out of trouble between now and then, and I wouldn't put it past Lamé to suspend key members of the team, as he'd threatened to do.

"Early Hump Day?" I texted him.

"Totally," he texted back.

I then texted Ellie, filling her in on our plans. You see, every week for as far back as I can remember, Levi, Ellie, and I have met at the boathouse for dinner, drinks, and a midweek unwind. This week, with the added pressure of athletes on a rampage and the summerlike weather, enjoying a BBQ and margaritas on the beach a day early seemed like just the ticket. I was pretty sure I had plenty of tequila, but I'd need to pick up some limes when I stopped at the farmers market for salad fixings and veggies to grill. As was our custom, Levi would bring the meat and Ellie the dessert.

"I nominate Zoe," I heard Hazel announce.

Nominate Zoe? I had obviously missed something while daydreams of pumpkin cheesecake and margaritas had been dancing through my mind.

"Nominate Zoe for what?" I took a risk and asked.

"Chairperson for next month's community dinner," Hazel answered.

"Oh, I don't know," I backpedaled. "You know I'm happy to help out, but chairperson?"

"Come on, Zoe, it's your turn and you know it," Willa pointed out.

"Yeah, but November is a really busy month for me," I tried.

"Busy how?" I knew Willa was like a dog with a bone once she'd made up her mind about something.

"Fall is mating season for many of our wildlife friends."

"And they somehow need your assistance?" Willa wasn't letting go.

"Well, not help exactly." I actually blushed. "It's just that . . ." Oh, hell.

"Okay, then, because Zoe will be busy helping our local wildlife 'get busy,'" Tawny laughed, "I'll take the community dinner next month and Zoe can take the Hometown Christmas in December."

Crap. "I'm sure the wildlife can get by on their own," I recanted my earlier objection. The Christmas event was ten times as much work as the community dinner. "I'll do the dinner."

"Too late." Tawny smiled. "I motion that Zoe and I switch. I'll take the dinner and Zoe can do Hometown Christmas."

"I second," Hazel joined in.

"No, don't second," I said. "The dinner is fine, really."

"All in favor?" Willa ignored me.

"Aye," everyone in the room except my dad, Levi, Ellie, and me answered.

"Opposed?" Willa asked.

"Nay," I stated loudly, while Dad, Ellie, and Levi backed me up in more demure tones.

"The motion is carried," Willa declared.

I groaned. When was I ever going to learn to keep my mouth shut? Ellie shot me a look of sympathy. She'd had to chair the event the previous year and knew what a nightmare it was. Truth be told, December is a slow month for me. The wildlife are mostly sleeping, few people bring their unwanted animals to the shelter right before Christmas, and those animals who are brought in are quickly adopted to dads and moms trying to grant the wishes of their little darlings who want Santa to bring them doggies or kitties this year.

"Don't worry. I'll be in town," Zak whispered in my ear. "I'll help you."

This day just keeps getting better and better.

Chapter 3

The Ashton Falls branch of the Timberland County Animal Shelter is housed in a large log structure shaped like a T. Charlie and I entered the lobby, which is located at the front of the stem of the T. Beyond the lobby is a long hallway with offices, exam rooms, and housing for cats and small animals both wild and domestic. Currently this section houses six cats, a raccoon with a broken leg, two cottontail bunnies that came out on the losing end of an altercation with a dog, and a ferret I suspect was someone's pet that got away.

When you get to the end of the hall you will find facilities for the dogs to the right —which include kennels with individual indoor/outdoor runs and a large common area—and wild animals to the left. The wild animal facility is divided into both large and small enclosures. At the far end is the roomiest structure, which is used to house larger wildlife such as our resident bear. Next to that are several smaller enclosures, which are currently occupied by two coyote pups I hope to release soon.

"Mrs. Watson called again," Jeremy commented as soon as I poured myself a cup of coffee. "She wants us to find a home for Kiva. Her daughter is coming up tomorrow to help her move into the retirement home."

"Okay, I'll pick him up this afternoon." I sorted through my mail and checked the corkboard for messages. I felt bad for Mrs. Watson. Kiva, a twelve-year-old yellow lab with a slight limp, was her pride and joy, and I knew she had fought her daughter tooth and nail on the family's decision to move her into an assisted-living facility that didn't allow dogs. Still, Mrs. Watson was getting on in years and, after a bad fall a couple of months back, she was having a hard time with the stairs leading up to her small house.

Ever since the poor woman first called me in tears, I had been thinking of potential homes for the hard-to-place dog. I needed to find someone kind and gentle who would be patient with the elderly canine; someone who would be willing to make the thirty-mile drive to take Kiva to visit Mrs. Watson every now and then. After a lot of thought and much consideration, I believed I'd found the perfect candidate, the most gentle and compassionate man I know, my dad.

"That Border collie we brought in a couple of weeks ago was finally adopted." Jeremy, a twenty-year-old, stick-thin heavy metal drummer with a nose ring and a neck tattoo, brushed his long brown hair out of his eyes as he handed me the adoption paperwork.

"That's good. I was beginning to worry about finding a home for such an active little dog." County regulations state that dogs and cats that remain unadopted after six weeks at the shelter must be sent to the main facility in the valley for "processing." (That's a pretty way of saying they're euthanized.) Since I technically work for the county, I'm supposed to adhere to that rule. Of course, pigs will fly before I send even one of my charges off to an untimely death, so Jeremy and I make it our mission to seek out matches for our orphans long before the six weeks approach. The average stay for any of our adoptees is less than two weeks unless medical conditions requiring monitoring and treatment dictate a longer visit.

"That only leaves us with four cats and three dogs to place," Jeremy added. "I'm confident we can find them homes at the adoption booth on Sunday. Once we release the bear cub and those coyote pups, things are going to be pretty quiet around here."

"Ideally," I agreed, "but unfortunately that isn't the way things usually work. I've been working here for eight years and have yet to have an empty facility. However, if we do end up with just four cats and three dogs for the pet adoption booth, let's see if we can get the main office to send up some of their short-timers."

"Ever worry about running out of folks to do the adopting?"

"I try never to worry about things I can't control," I answered. "I just take it one day at a time and hope for the best."

I began my shift as I do every day, with a slow drive through the alley parallel to the three-mile stretch of road known as Main Street. My focus is to pick up any new strays, wild or domesticated. After this task is completed, I move onto my other duties, which, on a normal day, consist of handling nuisance wildlife calls and answering complaints involving dog bites or noisy pets.

After finishing my sweep I headed over to Donovan's to ask my dad about Kiva. I'd meant to talk to him about it at the community events meeting, but he'd managed to slip out while I was talking to Hazel. I knew if I could assure Mrs. Watson that Kiva

41

would have a home with my dad, a man she liked and respected, the transition would be much easier on everyone.

Donovan's, like many of the mom-and-pop shops in Ashton Falls, is a hybrid store offering a variety of products for the home and outdoors. Originally built by my grandfather over forty years ago, the building, constructed entirely of logs milled locally, is laid out in a rectangular fashion with double-wide entry doors placed squarely in the middle. As you walk into the facility, you notice a large oak counter fashioned in a square, with a cash register in the center and an assortment of small items for sale on the other three countertops. Just to the left of the cashiers' station is an alcove with a potbellied stove. The alcove is furnished with three long sofas covered with a dark brown fabric and arranged in a U shape.

"Hey, Dad," I greeted him as I stooped down to pet Tucker, who had trotted over to greet Charlie and me. I waved at Nick Benson and Tanner Brown, two of the seniors in my book club, who were focused intently on a game of checkers. "I need a favor."

"What's its name?" My dad tossed Charlie a biscuit as he sat politely at his feet. After accepting the customary treat, Charlie and Tucker trotted over to join Nick and Tanner by the fire.

"How do you know that's the favor?" I leaned against the counter next to the register.

"Because," my dad said, beginning to refill display jars of penny candy, "you're a strong and independent woman who only ever asks me for one kind of help."

Dad was right. I do tend toward self-sufficiency, but I'm never too proud to beg, borrow, or steal in the mission of finding homes for the adorable creatures God has entrusted to me. "Mrs. Watson's daughter is putting her in a home. I need someone who's patient and understanding to take Kiva."

"When?"

"Today."

"Need me to pick him up?"

"That would be great." I couldn't help but sigh with relief. Deep down I knew my dad would come through—he always did—but I guess there was a tiny kernel of doubt burrowing in the back of my mind. "You could talk to Mrs. Watson and reassure her that Kiva will have a good home. I know this whole thing has been really hard on her. Kiva is her baby."

"I know." My dad came around from behind the counter and hugged me. "I'm proud of the way you work so hard to make sure everyone around you is taken care of. I'll head over there after closing."

"Thanks." I kissed my old man on the cheek. "I'll call and tell her you're coming. I love you, you know."

"I know. I love you, too. Dinner Friday?"

"Friday's the game," I reminded him. "How about Monday?"

"Monday's not good." He paused. "How about Tuesday?"

"Tuesday works."

"I heard about the trouble at the high school," Dad said, changing the subject.

"Yeah, Levi told me about the field and the jerseys. He said lamebrain is threatening to suspend anyone involved if the hijinks continue."

"Did he tell you about the truck?" Dad asked.

"Truck?"

"Someone decorated Coach Griswold's truck with colorful words written in colorful paint. Griswold is blaming the Bulldogs, although as far as I know he has no proof and every member of the team is denying it."

"Poor Levi. He's having a rough week."

"Yeah, and it might be getting a whole lot worse. I guess Griswold isn't giving up easily. He's telling anyone who will listen that he's going to make it his mission to see that Levi is fired over this incident. I hear Principal Lamé is considering a suspension."

"He wouldn't do that."

"Man's a stickler for the rules."

My dad was right. Suspending Levi before the big game and ruining our team's chance at a championship just to make a point sounded exactly like something lamebrain would do.

"Have you talked to Levi?" I wondered.

"No. Zak stopped by to see if I had anything he could use to clean up the field and we chatted for a spell. He convinced Levi that the best revenge is to beat the pants off the Beavers on Friday, so he volunteered to clean up the graffiti on the field while Levi works with his captains on their game plan."

I glanced at the clock; it was almost four. I'd managed to stop at the farmers market earlier in the day, but I still had a couple more errands before Levi and Ellie arrived for dinner in just over an hour. "Guess I should head out." I hugged my dad. "Thanks again for taking Kiva. I'm sure it'll mean a lot to Mrs. Watson."

"Happy to do it." My dad hugged me back.

Chapter 4

Charlie and I live in a converted boathouse that, along with fifty acres of lakefront property that goes with it, is owned by my maternal grandfather, who originally used it to house his boat. Nine years ago a group of farmers in the valley got together and challenged the legality of the Ashton Falls Dam, which had been built some forty years earlier by a group of recreationalists who wanted to raise the natural rim of the lake to better accommodate white-water rafting in the nearby Ashton River. At the time the dam was built water was plentiful and everyone was happy, but after seven years of drought the farm community at the foot of the mountain was looking for a way to force the transfer of a greater amount of the runoff from the mountains directly to their crops.

After winning what was at the time an extremely messy lawsuit, the farmers forced the opening of the dam and the water level decreased dramatically, effectively relocating the boathouse a good twenty feet from the natural waterline. Several years ago I asked my mom if it would be possible for me to convert the abandoned structure and, surprisingly, my grandfather not only agreed but offered to pay for the renovation as well. Charlie and I have been living there ever since.

I love my home. I mean, I really, really love it. It's weathered and unconventional, with a large living area, a small loft bedroom, and a modern yet cozy kitchen. The entire wall facing the lake has been replaced with glass to give the space an open, airy feel. Off the front of the boathouse is a large deck, where I love to while away a summer afternoon or entertain guests. The little cove the boathouse is built on is isolated from the main residential section of the lake, so when you're sitting on the deck it feels like you have the entire lake to yourself.

My dad's contribution to the remodel was a fantastic floor-to-ceiling river-rock fireplace built with stones he personally selected. The fireplace is built on the east wall of the structure, while the wall of windows faces south. Charlie and I adore curling by an inviting fire to watch the storms roll in over the distant mountain summit. Being warm and cozy inside while a storm rages outside gives us a feeling of comfort and contentment beyond description.

Today was sunny and not stormy, however, so I opted to forgo an indoor fire in favor of a fire in the pit on the beach that Levi helped me build two summers ago. After igniting the logs, I lit the charcoal for the BBQ, mixed up the first batch of frozen drinks, and settled onto one of the lounge chairs on the deck, waiting for my guests to arrive. Most evenings, if the wind is calm and the air warm, I kayak around my little cove and watch it get dark as the animals that live in the forest scurry into their shelters and homes.

Ellie was the first to show up. After pouring herself a margarita, she joined Charlie and me on the deck. "Fantastic weather for October," she commented as she twisted her straight brown hair into a knot and secured it on the back of her head with a clip. "In fact, it's actually a bit on the warm side, but I hear there's a storm blowing in by the end of next week." Her brown eyes danced with enthusiasm. "We might even get snow on the mountain. Is Levi going to show?"

"Yeah, but he might be late."

"It's been a tough week," Ellie sympathized.

"Did you hear about the incident with the Beavers' coach?" I asked.

"No. What happened?"

I filled Ellie in on everything my dad had shared with me. I could see the light fade from Ellie's eyes as I told her about Coach Griswold's vow to have Levi fired.

"We should talk to him," Ellie said.

"We might just make him madder. Maybe a night free of football is a better approach. Perhaps it would be best to talk about something else entirely."

"It'll come up," Ellie pointed out.

"Yeah, I guess. But we should try not to be preachy. Levi hates that."

Twenty minutes later, Levi showed up, with Zak and Lambda in tow. I wasn't thrilled about the extra guest but decided not to make an issue of it; apparently Levi and Zak had renewed their friendship, and it had never been a problem in the past to bring a friend or two along for Hump Day wind downs. Besides, I was thrilled to see Lambda, who ran over to greet me as soon as his feet hit the ground.

"I ran into Zak and invited him along." Levi handed me a large butcher-wrapped package. "I figured you had enough food for one more, but I brought a couple of extra steaks just in case."

"I'll take those," Ellie volunteered, hugging both men and inviting them in to make drinks.

Levi and Ellie played with the dogs on the beach while I began mixing another pitcher of drinks, and Zak took over the grilling of the steaks.

"It looks like Lambda is happy to be home," I commented as we watched the dogs running up and down the beach, chasing the balls Levi and Ellie were throwing.

"Yeah, the traveling was hard on him. I think we're going to settle down and stay home for a while. I heard your grandfather's estate is for sale. I thought I might look into buying it."

The estate Zak was referring to was located just around the bend, where the cove I live on opens up to the rest of the lake. By highway the two properties are separated by a good quarter mile, but the distance by beach is barely a hop, a skip, and a jump.

Zak and me neighbors? The idea didn't thrill me. Still, Zak was better than some unknown millionaire who could close off access to the lake, as some isolationists were known to do.

"The last time I talked to my mom she said my grandfather was thinking of selling, but I didn't realize he had actually listed it."

"He hasn't. At least not officially," Zak explained. "Your dad told me that he was thinking of selling, so I called and talked to him about it."

"My dad knew he wanted to sell?" This surprised me; my dad and my grandfather never talked to each other. I mean *ever*.

"Your mom mentioned it to him."

"My mom?" I wasn't aware that my mom and dad even acknowledged each other's existence on the planet. My mom certainly never mentioned my dad to me during our infrequent visits, and I was obsessively careful never to mention his name to her. Likewise, my dad and I never talked about Mom or her family in even the most casual way.

"I guess they had dinner or something. Anyway, the mansion is just sitting vacant, and I figured it'd be a lot quicker and easier to buy it than to start from scratch with new construction. I'm meeting with your grandfather's representative tomorrow to take a tour and discuss a deal. If it all works out, we could be neighbors by the time the first snow falls."

"Dinner?" I have to confess I had stopped listening the minute Zak mentioned that my parents had had dinner together.

"Come again?"

"You said my parents had dinner," I emphasized.

"That's what your dad told me. Try to keep up," Zak teased. "Did you hear anything else I said?"

"My mother, Madison Montgomery, had dinner with my father, Hank Donovan?" No matter how many times I said it, I was having a hard time wrapping my head around the idea.

"I guess. So?"

"And he thought to mention it to you, but even though I saw him just this afternoon, he failed to mention it to me?"

"I'm sure it was no big deal. It just came up in conversation."

"No big deal? Are you kidding me?" I screeched.

As far as I knew, my mom and dad hadn't spoken since the day my mom left me with my dad. Even visitation with my mom was arranged through one of my grandfather's flunkies. I thought about the plans my dad had for Monday night and wondered if they were with my mom. The very idea that they were seeing one another totally blew my mind. Though they had been in love once. I supposed it wasn't inconceivable that the long-dormant flame could have reignited if they had happened to run into one another.

"I don't know all the details," Zak explained. "I stopped to talk to your dad while I was picking up supplies to clean up the field. I mentioned that I was thinking about finding a lakefront I could move into right away rather than waiting for one to be built. He mentioned that he'd run into your mom, who mentioned that your grandfather was thinking about selling. That's all I know. I swear."

"I thought my mom was in Europe. She's engaged to some prince or sheikh or something."

"She changed her mind." Zak shrugged. "Your dad said she decided that marriage to a prince wasn't really for her. She rented a cottage on the beach."

"My mother is living in Ashton Falls?" I knew my voice sounded all high and squeaky, but I found Zak's news simply unbelievable. Why hadn't she gotten hold of me? Why hadn't my dad told me she was back? Why had she rented a cottage when a perfectly good house had been standing totally empty for years at a time? And why did Zak know so much about what was going on in her life while I, her one and only daughter, was completely in the dark? I knew if I didn't get a grip, big baby tears were going to trickle down my face, and there was no way I was giving Zak the satisfaction of seeing me cry. My mom and I weren't super close, but still…

"She probably just wanted to get settled in before she called you." Zak didn't sound convincing, but he topped off my drink and turned his back to flip the steaks. "These are about done. Why don't you call the others and I'll get the salad and bread?"

Once everything was set out, we gathered around the large pine table in the far corner of the deck and chatted about a little of this and a little of that as we ate. Maybe it was the margaritas, but it seemed like Zak was going out of his way to be sweet and funny, and his sugar and nice wasn't annoying me nearly as much as it usually did. Besides, Zak's endless string of jokes and funny stories had both Levi and Ellie in stitches, and it did my heart good to see my two very best friends so happy and relaxed.

By the time we finished eating the sun was setting behind the distant mountain. Ellie and I cleared the dishes and put away the food while Levi and Zak threw a few more logs on the fire in the pit on the beach. The dogs, exhausted from their earlier romp, curled up for a nap while Levi sat on a log strumming his guitar and Ellie and I talked about the upcoming community picnic. Zak was unusually quiet, and I couldn't help but wonder what was on his mind.

As the hours passed and the air grew cold, we gathered our belongings and headed inside. I halfheartedly offered coffee, but what I really wanted was to put on my pj's and curl up with my thoughts. Luckily, my guests feigned fatigue, leaving me alone to process what Zak had shared.

I snuggled into the sofa in front of the fireplace and tried to wrap my head around the fact that my mom was not only back from Europe but had been living in the same town as me and no one, including my dad, whom up until a few hours ago I believed kept no secrets, had bothered to tell me. The whole thing made no sense.

My dad and mom met one summer while she was "roughing it" with her family at the lake house. I think it's important to understand that my mother is from money. A lot of it. And we aren't talking crisp, new, technology-generated riches; we're talking about an old and dusty fortune as tarnished and moldy as the outdated aristocrats who own it. My mother, who had been brought up in the midst of coming out parties, afternoon teas, world travel, country clubs, and private schools, was eighteen and going through what can only be termed a rebellious phase when my handsome, rugged father wandered into her life.

According to my father's admittedly embellished account, he'd been trolling the lake for fish when he'd seen the most breathtaking image on the beach, silhouetted by the setting sun. He told me that he knew in an instant that the vision in white was his one and only true love; the mother of his child; the master of his destiny. Sound a bit fantastic? You bet, but my father is a romantic, and I think he really did love her in that moment. He claims he tossed his anchor, dove overboard, and swam to shore, where he lifted her petite form into his large arms and kissed her like something out of a steamy romance novel. My mother apparently was both impressed and intrigued by his bold move, and I was born ten months later.

Although my father's telling of his first meeting with my mother seems more like a fantasy than a realistic rendition of an actual encounter, I completely believe the next part, where my uptight and stodgy grandparents found out that my mother was pregnant and shipped her off to an "aunt's" where I quietly, under the shroud of absolute secrecy, was delivered into the world. My grandparents wanted an anonymous adoption, but my dad fought hard and convinced them that he would raise me in isolation from the judgmental eyes of their aristocratic friends.

I don't remember a lot about the first four years of my life, but I do know that other than those first few days I had no contact with my mother whatsoever. Then, for reasons unbeknownst to me, when I was four my mother's maternal instinct kicked in and my father was notified through my grandfather's representative that my mother wanted to set up a visit. My father agreed, and I was escorted to a huge and intimidating estate, where I cowered in the closet in spite of my mother's clumsy attempt to parent me, until someone took mercy on me and returned me to my dad, the only parent I'd ever known.

The strange thing is, this truly horrifying experience planted a seed deep within my heart that germinated and grew into a desire that, I have to admit, I've never completely overcome. Until that point I'd never thought much about my family structure. I knew I had a dad while other kids had both a dad and a mom, but I'd never stopped to consider an alternative until I learned that I actually *did* have a mother, as scary as she might be. My idea flourished into a wish, which became an obsession. Every night before bed I uttered a prayer that always ended with "please bring me a mom who loves me and a brother or sister to play with." Eventually I met Levi and Ellie, and the brother or sister part seemed less urgent, but a mother? I guess in many ways I'm still waiting.

Chapter 5

Wednesday turned out to be a strange day. One of the strangest I'd had for quite some time.

The day started off, as do most of my days on the mountain, peaceful and calm, in the presence of nature and good friends. Charlie and I went for our early morning run, first along the lakeshore as we greeted the sunrise and galloped among the geese, then through the densely forested footpath that led to the marina at the north end of town. As we ran along the main street of Ashton Falls, we waved to proprietors just opening their shops, stopping briefly to talk to a few, but never very many and never for very long. As we neared the south end of town we veered slightly to the left, once again taking to the forest trail blanketed with the yellow leaves of autumn as the days shortened and winter neared.

After we got back to the boathouse I fed the animals and then showered while the coffee dripped. After dressing casually in jeans and my official county shirt over a black tank, I sat down on the railing of the deck overlooking the lake and watched the forest come to life for yet another day. It wasn't until Jeremy called just as I was turning onto the highway that things started to gently merge toward the bizarre.

"Mrs. Pansy called," Jeremy informed me. "Said Sadie is up a tree and can't get down."

"Up a tree?" I questioned. Sadie is Mrs. Pansy's dog, some totally unidentifiable mixed breed of nonspecific origin.

"That's what she said. I can head over if you want."

"No, I'm not far from there now. I'll check it out on my way into work."

I've been working with animal control and rescue for a long time. I started off as a volunteer when I was still in high school and have continued on as an employee; first part-time during summer breaks when I was in college, and now as the county director for the Ashton Falls facility. I've seen a lot during those years, but I have to admit that this was the first time I'd ever come across a dog up a tree. It looked like the Halloween hijinks were starting early this year.

When I arrived at Mrs. Pansy's home I verified that Jeremy had been correct; there was indeed a dog in a tree. A very frightened dog, by the look of things.

"She do this often?" I asked Mrs. Pansy.

"No. Never. I didn't even know dogs could climb trees."

I studied the area. The tree in question was easier than most to climb. In fact, it was just the type of tree I would never have been able to resist when I was a child. There were low branches that served as a base from which to access higher limbs that were conveniently spaced for maximum access. Sadie was perched on a branch about twelve feet off the ground in a bowl-shaped area where several branches met to form a perch of sorts. I realized that the only way the silly dog was going to get down was if I climbed up and got her.

I set my gear on the ground and started up the tree. Sadie was making the most god-awful noise that sounded like a cross between a howl and a screech. I forced myself to ignore the intense desire to cover my ears as I methodically climbed higher and higher. There's a certain rush that can be had climbing a tree. Much of my childhood was spent high atop the branches of the trees that surrounded the cabin where Dad and I lived while I was growing up. As I inched my way toward Sadie, I remembered the feeling of freedom that can be found thirty or forty feet above the ground. My dad used to say that if he couldn't find me, the first place he looked was up.

I focused my attention on the tree I was scaling. As I looked up into the branches dappled with sunlight, I smiled. In another situation I might have explored the limits presented by this specific tree, but poor Sadie looked scared to death. I was afraid she was going to take matters into her own metaphorical hands and jump before I could reach her and lower her safely to the ground, so I set my own yearnings aside and focused all my attention on the dog.

"I'm coming to get you, sweetie." I tried for a calm and soothing voice, which I realized was never going to be heard over Sadie's caterwauling. "Stupid dog," I said louder. "The first rule of tree climbing is never to climb up a tree you can't climb down."

Sadie stopped howling long enough to look at me. I guess that got her attention. "I'm going to move to the branch just below you," I explained, certain that she understood. "Once I get my footing, I'm going to lift you off the branch and tuck you into my shirtfront. It's important that you not wiggle around. Capiche?"

Apparently Sadie did, because other than a quick lick to the cheek, she followed my directions to a T.

"Oh, thank you!" Mrs. Pansy grabbed Sadie the moment my feet hit the ground. "I can't imagine how she got up there."

"Yeah." I glanced at a pair of tweens watching and laughing from across the street. "I can't imagine."

Several hours later I was cruising the alley behind the shops on Main Street looking for Dumpster dogs when I noticed Pack Rat Nelson sorting through the garbage behind Second Hand Suzie's. Pack Rat, so nicknamed due to his propensity for collecting *everything*, waved to me as I slowly neared. Pulling my truck next to the stout man with the bulbous nose and bloodshot eyes, I smiled at him in response to his toothless grin and asked how he was doing.

"Can't complain," he grunted. "You find a home for that mutt I brought into the shelter a few days ago?"

"I did. I meant to stop by and thank you, by the way. Poor little guy had an intestinal blockage. He would have died if you hadn't rescued him."

"Glad to help." Pack Rat picked up a lamp that was broken at the base and gently set it into his shopping cart. "I normally leave those who want to live on the streets to themselves, but the dog was moving slow and I was afraid if I didn't bring him in Sasquatch would get him."

"Sasquatch?"

"Seen it every night for the past week or so. Comes out after dark."

"Are you sure you haven't been seeing a bear? They've been extra-active lately." While we don't have grizzlies in our area, our black bear population is both plentiful and dynamic. Every year, once the

58

weather starts to cool, the bears enter into a feeding frenzy in preparation for hibernation, and the dumpsters along Main Street become a smorgasbord of cubby delight.

"No," Pack Rat insisted. "Not a bear."

"Can you describe what you saw?" I asked. On one hand, Pack Rat has a strange hobby, but as far as I knew he wasn't crazy. If he said he saw something, I'd be willing to bet he had.

"Tall, broad shouldered, face like a gorilla, body like a man. I know what you're thinking, but I really did see it. I was looking for scraps behind the lumberyard when I saw a kitten scramble under a woodpile. I was following the kitten to the back of the lot where its mom and siblings were hiding when I saw something coming from out of the woods. I scrunched down behind some logs, but I got a good look at it."

"Do you think it saw you?" I asked. I made a mental note to check on the kittens. If I could capture both the kittens and the mother, I could find homes for them where they would be safe from the coyotes that blanket this area. The fact of the matter is, our feral cat population is close to nonexistent due to the large number of natural predators.

"No," Pack Rat responded. "It was pretty intent on heading wherever it was it was going. He pretty much kept his head down."

"And he was heading to the alley behind Main Street?" I clarified.

"Yup. I followed him for a spell, but I tripped over an old soda bottle, and I'm afraid that got his attention. I took off real quick like."

Pack Rat picked up a discarded fork and wiped it clean on his stained overalls. He held up the fork to the light for a better look. Satisfied with what he saw, he placed the fork in his pocket.

"If you see Sasquatch again, will you let me know?" I requested. It wasn't that I was worried that the *real* Sasquatch was prowling around Ashton Falls, but if we had a nuisance animal, I felt it best that we dealt with it sooner rather than later.

Pack Rat shrugged but didn't say anything. I handed him $20. "A reward for bringing in the sick dog," I informed him. "Thanks again. Oh, and about those kittens," I added, as I placed the truck into drive. "I really should pick them up and find them homes before the coyotes get them. Can you remember how many there were?"

Pack Rat paused. I knew he was trying to decide whether or not to help me with the kittens. I understood his philosophy that both people and animals should be allowed to live as they saw fit, but I also knew the kittens would never make it into adulthood if left to fend for themselves.

"They're too little to take care of themselves," I reminded him.

"Four," he finally answered. "There were four. One orange, two black, and one gray and white."

"Thanks." I smiled at the man. "I appreciate your help."

"The orange one is tricky," he warned. "Gonna be hard to catch him."

"I'll see what I can do, and if I can't get him, maybe you can help me later. After lunch." I glanced at the twenty he still clutched in his hand.

Pack Rat looked at the money in his hand and headed down the alley toward Jim's Taco Hut.

I radioed Jeremy to let him know I was going to head over to the lumberyard in the hope of locating and capturing the kittens. If I could catch the mom, I would. Feral cats rarely made good pets and are hard to place, but maybe the poor mom hadn't been on her own for long and was still salvageable. If not, I'd try to find a placement for her on one of the ranches in the valley, where there were mild winters and plenty of barns to hide in.

"How'd you do?" Jeremy asked as I walked in the door of the shelter an hour later with the five cats in a crate and Charlie on my heels.

"Got 'em all. The mom seems friendly enough. I'm betting she had a home and either wandered off or was abandoned. Let's put out a standard notification in case she's simply lost. The kittens are about four weeks old. We'll keep mom and kittens together a couple more weeks and then start looking for homes for them if no one claims them."

"Tawny Upton is looking for a kitten for Emily," Jeremy informed me. "She was in a few days ago and asked me to keep an eye out for one. I guess she promised Emily she could have her own cat when she turned ten."

"Give her a call." I released the mom and kittens into a large holding pen, where they would have plenty of room to wander around. "Do we still have that bedding we used for the Doberman puppies?" I asked.

"Yeah, I washed it and put it in the storeroom. I'll get it."

"Grab a litter box while you're in there," I suggested. I stopped to cradle and caress each of our new residents as I placed them into the pen. The mom actually looked relieved that someone was helping out, if it was possible for a cat to look relieved. She began to purr, confirming my suspicion that she hadn't been on the street long. I hoped we'd find her owner, but if not, I had several seniors in mind who might welcome an adult cat into their homes.

I sorted through the messages on my desk as I waited for Jeremy to return with the stuff from the storage room. The Bryton Lake shelter had three dogs they desperately needed to place and wondered if we could find homes for them. I never turn down an animal on the short list for disposal, so I made a note to call them and arrange for a pickup.

"Have you heard anything about Sasquatch sightings?" I asked Jeremy when he returned to the office.

"Sasquatch?" Jeremy looked at me like I'd lost my mind.

"I had a conversation with Pack Rat earlier, and he mentioned seeing Sasquatch several times during the past week."

"Probably a bear."

"Yeah, that's what I thought. Still, it occurred to me that with the rash of break-ins we've been having, maybe what he really saw was our local thief."

"Could be." Jeremy shrugged, "By the way, Zak came by. He brought Lambda. It was good to see them both. He mentioned he was looking into buying a house and staying around for a while."

"Yeah," I said vaguely. I didn't want to rehash my feelings about Zak's return to the area with Jeremy.

For one thing, what I had thought were strong feelings of repulsion for the guy were becoming inexplicably muddied with something so closely akin to fondness that it was totally freaking me out.

"He offered to help out with the pet adoption booth at the community picnic on Sunday and I took him up on it. I figured it'd be nice to have the extra help. We're going to need a few more pets, though."

"I'm going to drive over to Bryton Lake after lunch and pick up a couple of short- timers. I'll see what they have. Maybe I can bring a few additional adoptees as well."

"Speaking of Bryton Lake, Levi called. He wanted you to get back to him before you left. He said it was important."

"Why didn't he just call me on my cell?"

"He did. He said he left a message, as well as a text, but you didn't respond."

I took my phone out of my pocket and realized I'd left it on silent. According to Levi's text, he needed me to execute an urgent and sensitive favor. I had to admit he had my interest.

"I'm going to head over to the high school," I informed Jeremy. "They should let out for lunch in fifteen minutes or so. I'll see what Levi wants and then head over to Bryton Lake." I switched my cell from silent to ring. "I'm leaving Charlie with you since I'm not sure how long I'll be at the school. Call me if anything comes up."

Chapter 6

"So what's so urgent?" I asked Levi twenty minutes later.

"I'm afraid there's a new victim in the tug-of-war between the Bulldogs and the Beavers; Popeye is missing."

"They stole Popeye?" I couldn't believe what I was hearing. Kidnapping the Bulldog mascot would be a low blow.

"It appears so," Levi confirmed. "Kyle Green said he let him out into his backyard this morning, but when he went to let him back in he was gone. The guys are sure the Beavers have him."

"This prank thing has gone way too far. We should tell Lamé."

"We can't. If we do, we'll have to admit our part in the incident and Lamé will most likely fire me and suspend the boys."

"Your part?"

"The Bulldogs stole Benny's head."

I knew that Benny was a giant beaver costume worn by one of the members of the Beaver's pep squad during football games. I tried to wrap my head around the absurdity of the situation. Stolen costume? Missing dog? What was the world coming to?

"I need you to arrange for a swap," Levi said.

"Me?"

"Lamé has already threatened dire consequences if anyone associated with the team is seen within thirty miles of Bryton Lake. I've arranged for you to meet one of the guys from the team and make the switch; their costume for our dog."

I hesitated. I guess it wouldn't hurt to help Levi out since I was going to Bryton Lake to pick up the shelter animals anyway. "Okay, what do you want me to do?"

After getting specific directions from Levi, I returned to my truck and headed down the mountain. Bryton Lake is a middle-class town wrapped in an upper-class package. The entire town, as well as the high school, has undergone a major redevelopment in an attempt to bring in higher-end tourists. A huge outlet mall was built to replace the mom- and-pop shops that once lined the downtown corridor; fine dining establishments have replaced fast-food chains; the old high school was renamed Bryton Lake Academy, giving the old school an elegant feel.

I parked my truck in the back lot where there was more room to maneuver. I noticed Coach Griswold's recently vandalized truck near the new auto shop. When my dad mentioned that Griswold's truck had been tagged, I assumed it was part of the rivalry between the football teams, but as I read the graffiti I realized my assumption might have been premature. I expected to find tags like BULLISH ON BULLDOGS or BEAVERS ARE DAMMED. Instead the graffiti conveyed a totally different and much more disturbing type of message. I took a photo of the damaged truck with my phone and continued on toward the meeting place behind the shop buildings, where Levi had indicated I was to meet the team member who would make the swap.

"Cody Blunt?" I asked the boy loitering behind the metal shop.

"You bring the costume?" he asked.

"If you brought the dog," I countered.

"In the van." The boy with the dirty blond hair nodded toward a white cargo van that had seen better days.

"My truck is around front."

The boy looked nervous, too nervous. We were, after all, simply exchanging goods procured by a friendly pregame raid and not engaging in international espionage.

"Griswold see you?" The boy wiped beads of sweat from his brow even though the temperature was quite mild.

I shrugged. "His truck is in the lot, but I didn't see him. I'm not sure if he saw me. That's quite some paint job someone did on his ride."

The boy's eyes filled with panic and I began to wonder if the graffiti on the truck had anything to do with the pregame hijinks. The taunts were dark and extremely disturbing.

"You on the team?" I asked.

"Mascot," the boy confirmed.

"So it's your costume that's missing."

"Look, I'm toast if I don't get it back. Can we make the switch?"

"Yeah, okay," I replied. "How do you want to do this?"

The boy nervously scanned the area. "Too many people around. I'll meet you at the intersection just outside the front gate."

I shrugged. "Okay, I'll be there in five."

I played my conversation with Cody over and over in my mind as I walked back to my truck. The kid seemed scared, and not in an I-screwed-up-and-I-might-get-detention way. If I had to guess, I'd say he was being abused by someone. The question was who. Griswold? He seemed the likely candidate, although his fear of losing the beaver costume could have been generated by a parent or teammate.

The switch went smoothly. I rescued Popeye, picked up five dogs and three cats from the Bryton Lake shelter, and returned home with my task completed but my psyche disturbed.

"This little guy is exactly what Nick Benson has been looking for," Jeremy commented as he helped me unload and settle our newest residents. "I'll call him when we're done here."

I was still thinking about Cody Blunt's haunted eyes and didn't respond, which was unusual; I'm normally a regular chatterbox.

"Everything okay?" Jeremy asked.

"I'm not sure." I pulled out my phone and showed him the photo of Coach Griswold's truck. "Does this look like pregame hijinks to you?"

Jeremy frowned. "Not really. It looks more like payback for something pretty heinous. Did you show this to Levi?"

"Not yet, but I will. I had the feeling the kid I met to make the switch was terrified."

"You think Griswold is abusing his kids?"

"I don't know. Maybe. Or maybe someone else associated with the team. I hate to start making accusations when I have so little to go on."

"Yeah, you'd better be sure before you say anything," Jeremy agreed.

After getting the dogs settled, Charlie and I decided to stop by the haunted barn to see if event coordinator Joel Ringer had any extra zombies we could borrow for the run on Saturday. It occurred to me that because the run was scheduled in the morning and the haunted barn didn't open until later in the afternoon, there might be a brain sucker or two who would be willing to do double duty.

The haunted barn was held in an actual barn located just outside of town. One of the advantages of using the barn as a haunted house was that it was pretty darn spooky on its own, requiring little in the way of decoration. Real cobwebs hung from dusty rafters that could be accentuated with artificial cobwebs bearing real spiders. Imitation walls were erected to create narrow spaces and multiple rooms. The barn didn't open for another hour, but there was already a line snaking through the graveyard and down the narrow dirt road leading to the main highway.

Charlie and I had no desire to wait for the event to open so we skirted the line and headed toward a side door.

"Hey, Zoe, what brings you out?" Joel asked as Charlie and I entered the building.

"What happened to this place?" The entire room was covered with graffiti.

"Looks like the Halloween Hijinks started early this year. It appears a group of kids broke in last night," Joel said. "At least I assume it was kids. I don't really see adults doing something like this. Not only was the lock broken and the walls tagged with colorful epitaphs but there was an assortment of beer bottles all over the floor."

"What are you going to do?"

"I fixed the lock, picked up the beer bottles, and decided to incorporate the graffiti into the design. I painted over all the more graphic words and pictures."

"Good thinking." I was impressed at Joel's ability to keep his cool in the face of the vandalism. I walked to the wall and considered the artwork. I was certain at least some of the comments had been painted by the same person or persons who had tagged Griswold's truck. The lettering used on some of the words was distinctive in design.

"And you have no idea who might have done this?" I asked.

"Not a clue. I heard about the break-ins in town and thought it could be related, but after I thought about it, it seemed like my intruders were after a cool place to party rather than merchandise of any type."

"Was anything taken?"

"Not as far as I can tell. So what can I do for you and Charlie?"

"We wanted to ask you about borrowing some of your zombies for the run Saturday morning. I'm afraid with the game the day before, the football players are totally focused on decimating Bryton Lake and only a few have signed up."

"I should have a few guys willing to help you out. What time do you need them?"

"Seven?" I knew that was early for the walking dead and was afraid the early start would scare off potential runners. "Seven-thirty if they show up already in makeup."

"The haunted barn goes until after midnight on Friday night, so I'm not sure how many volunteers I'll get, but I'll certainly ask."

"Thanks." I smiled.

"Let me show you the new mechanics I've been working on," Joel offered.

I followed him to the back of the barn where a drop-down ladder hung from the loft above. I told Charlie to stay before climbing up after him. I was more than a little surprised by the amount of equipment needed to pull off the spooky spectacular.

"Wow. I had no idea so much went into this." I was honestly impressed.

"It's quite a production." Joel grinned. "Check this out." He pushed a series of buttons and the dummies below came to life. I laughed as Charlie began barking at a mechanical skeleton on the floor below us.

"We were able to add a torture chamber this year with the money we had left from last year's production," Joel proudly informed me. "The blood may be fake, but I guarantee this room is going to terrify even the most skeptical reveler. Come on, I'll show you."

I followed Joel past signs warning that children and those with health conditions should avoid the exhibit. It looked like this year's haunted barn was going to be the best one ever.

After leaving the barn, Charlie and I decided to stop by the hospital to visit Warren Trent. Ashton Falls Community Hospital is little more than a clinic where minor injuries and routine surgeries are attended to, saving the citizens of our community a trip down the mountain to the larger hospital in the metropolis below.

"Afternoon, Zoe, Charlie," Dr. Ryder Westlake greeted us. Dr. Westlake was not only a babe but an all-around nice guy as well. If it weren't for his support, Charlie's desire to volunteer as a therapy dog would never have seen fruition. "Are you here to do the therapy thing?"

"Sort of," I responded. "Charlie and I thought we'd drop in on Warren Trent. How's he doing?"

"Not as well as I'd hoped, I'm afraid. It looks like he's going to need surgery." Dr. Westlake's bright green eyes revealed genuine concern. "Without it, the bone might not heal the way we'd like. He's too young to struggle with a limp for the rest of his life."

"That's too bad," I said. "Will you need to send him down the mountain?"

"Yes, he'll need to see a specialist." I followed Dr. Westlake's strong hand as he ran it through his dark brown hair. I'd noticed similar behavior when he had a problem that didn't sit quite right. "I'm sure he'll welcome a visit, though. If we can work out the details, we'll transport him down the mountain before the weekend."

"Okay, then, we'll head back. It was good talking to you."

"Next time you come to do a therapy session let me know," he added as I turned to walk away. "I'd like to sit in."

"Okay, I will." I smiled.

"Zoe, what are you doing here?" Warren asked as Charlie and I continued down the hall and entered his room.

"Charlie wanted to come by and say hi."

"I'm thrilled for the company. I asked the doc if my dad could bring my dog by but was told that hospital policy doesn't allow pets."

"Charlie is a certified therapy dog," I explained.

"Hey, Charlie." Warren tried to lean over the side of the bed to get a better look at him, but his leg was in a sling that hung from a rod over the bed, making it almost impossible to do so. "Can he come up?"

"Charlie, up," I patted the bed and commanded.

Charlie carefully leapt up onto the bed, settling next to Warren's arm on his uninjured side. Warren grinned as Charlie carefully laid his head on Warren's stomach and let him pet his head.

"Did you find out anything more about who did this to you?" I sat down in a chair next to the bed.

"All I remember is a white truck. It was getting dark and I was in a hurry to get home after practice. The whole thing happened so fast. I was lucky I had time to swerve. The guy could have killed me."

"So it was a man driving?"

Warren frowned as he thought about it. "Yeah, it was. Tall, dark hair, some sort of hat. Maybe a baseball cap? You know, I didn't remember any of this until this moment."

"Happens that way sometimes," I explained.

"I didn't see his face at all, though. Like I said, it was getting dark and his headlights blinded me. I'm lucky to be alive, although I'm pretty upset about missing the game on Friday. The team was counting on me."

I didn't know what to say. The team *was* counting on him. He was the best player they had. There was little chance they were going to win without him, and we both knew it. I struggled to come up with something witty or at least comforting.

"How's the food?" I asked when I drew a blank.

"Terrible."

"Are you on a restricted diet?"

"I'm not sure. Based on the crap they've been feeding me, I'd guess yes, though."

"Let me see what I can do. Charlie, stay," I instructed as I slipped out the door.

Luckily, Doctor Gorgeous hadn't left yet and I was able to get permission to bring Warren anything he wanted to eat. When I returned to Warren's room he told me he'd kill for a pizza, so I had one delivered, along with a six pack of soda, then Charlie and I sat with him while he ate his dinner and told us stories of his best football plays from the past. By the time we left, he was nodding off from the pain killers the nurse had brought in after he finished his meal.

Chapter 7

The next morning I saw Ellie exiting the Ashton Falls Community Bank as I made my rounds along Main Street. I knew that a prime storefront had become available on the pier near Timberland Beach, and Ellie and her mother were trying to secure the necessary funding to open a soup and sandwich shop there. The facility wasn't large enough to house an industrial kitchen, so their idea was to sell cold sandwiches, salads, and soup premade in Rosie's main kitchen to the crowd who gathered at the lake during the warm summer months. There was a large deck area where they planned to set up an outdoor patio, as well as several BBQs where they could grill ribs, chicken, and hamburgers made to order.

During the winter, when the beach crowd had migrated indoors and the cross- country ski mob overran the beach, they planned to convert the sandwich and BBQ shop into a warming hut specializing in hot beverages, both with and without alcohol, as well as homemade soup, bread, muffins, and other sweet treats.

"So?" I pulled over in front of the bank. "How'd it go?"

Ellie reached inside the passenger window to pet Charlie. "Good, I think. Blakely," she said, referring to the bank president, "wants me to submit a formal business plan complete with a sample menu for both summer and winter. He also wants me to bring in some samples."

"Samples?"

"Of the soup we plan to serve, mainly. He says the samples will help him evaluate the potential success of the enterprise but if you want my opinion, I think he just wants a free lunch."

I laughed. I had to agree with Ellie's assessment of Blakely's true intent. He was a portly man who loved to eat but was also famous for being a tightwad of the tightest kind. If he could find a way to dine for free, he wasn't too embarrassed to take it. "So are you going to do it?"

"Of course," Ellie replied. "If a couple of servings of soup will get us the loan we need, I'm happy to oblige. Now I just need to figure out which soups to bring."

"Your shrimp chowder for sure," I suggested. "And Levi swears by your beef stew. Oh, and your cheesy chicken chowder is to die for. Darn, now I'm hungry."

"Mom made soup this morning. I think todays specials are Timberland Shrimp Chowder and Pizza in a Pot. Come on over and grab a bowl."

"I need to finish rounds.. How about if I get there around eleven-thirty?"

"I'll see you then." Ellie waved and continued down the street.

Charlie and I continued on our rounds, but I knew we were both trying to figure out which of Rosie's soups we'd try for lunch. I was leaning toward the shrimp chowder, but I was pretty sure Charlie would prefer the Pizza in a Pot. Maybe I'd have to turn a blind eye and let him have a small bowl of that.

The morning continued smoothly enough. I slowly drove my familiar route, keeping an eye out for stray animals. Most times if there was a homeless pup on the loose, I'd find him or her scavenging garbage from the Dumpsters that lined the alley behind the main drag. During the summer months, when the beaches were crowded with families sharing picnics on the warm sand, the homeless animal population tended to gravitate toward the shoreline along the lake.

I decided to stop and check in on Gilda Reynolds, owner of Bears and Beavers Gift Shop. Gilda is short and stout with bright red hair that she wears naturally in a sort of frizzy Afro. One of the biggest contributors to the town, she serves on several community groups, including the First Baptist Coats for Kids Coalition and the Timberland Mountain Arts Project, in addition to the Ashton Falls Events Committee.

Gilda recently had adopted a chocolate lab that was exhibiting severe anxiety any time she was left alone. She'd tried numerous "remedies" as suggested by friends and family, but nothing seemed to be working. The last time I'd talked to her, she was close to throwing in the towel and asking me to find Hershey another home. While I didn't disagree that Hershey might be happier in a situation where her owner was a little less busy, I also felt that with time and patience on Gilda's part, she and Hershey could be very happy.

"Hey, Gilda," I greeted as I walked into the quaint mountain shop. "I thought I'd stop by and check on Hershey."

The dog looked up from the corner where she'd been napping when she heard her name. She really was a sweet dog, and generally well behaved, but every time Gilda left her alone in the house, she went just a little bit nuts. I had to admit Gilda had been more than patient with the emotionally damaged dog. If she left Gilda in a crate, she howled the entire time she was gone, earning her the wrath of her closet neighbors, and if she left her free in the house, Hershey chewed on anything and everything she could find to destroy.

"She's doing better since I started bringing her with me to work," Gilda answered my unspoken question. "We've settled into an agreement of sorts where I take her where I can and she behaves when I have to leave her. I've been thinking about getting another dog to keep her company. I watched my daughter's little terrier for a few days while she was out of town and Hershey tended to do better."

"It might help," I agreed. "If you want, I'll keep an eye out for a good match and let you have him or her on a trial basis before committing to the adoption."

"That would be great."

"I heard you had a visit from the random bandit," I added. I had to admit the antics of this particular late-night stalker had captured my attention.

"Random is right. I don't really get this guy. He breaks in, takes a beaver cookie jar and a set of coffee mugs with bears on them, doesn't even touch the cash I'd left in the till, and then locks the door when he leaves."

"You left cash in the till?" I asked.

"Sometimes I forget to put it in the safe," Gilda admitted. "I've never had a problem before."

"Maybe the thief didn't realize there was cash in the register."

"Maybe," Gilda acknowledged. "But it still seems odd that he took a few inexpensive items and left a whole store full of much more expensive merchandise untouched."

"Yeah, that does seem odd," I agreed. "It seems like that's his pattern. The whole thing is bizarre."

By the time I finally made it to Rosie's the lunch crowd had begun to gather. Ellie was busy in the kitchen, so I placed my order and settled onto one of the pine benches on the patio. It was a nice day for late October, but a bit on the chilly side for most, so Charlie and I ended up having the whole deck to ourselves. After I finished off a huge bowl of shrimp chowder, it occurred to me that Warren might appreciate a decent meal as well. I called the hospital and verified that his dietary restrictions hadn't changed before calling him on his cell phone and getting his order.

"I'm so glad you called." Warren grinned as Charlie and I walked through the door of his hospital room carrying a take-out bag that contained a double cheeseburger and fries. "The staff has been super nice, but I'm pretty sure they're trying to starve me."

"Any idea when you'll be moved down the mountain for surgery?" I pulled a table over to Warren's bed and set the bag where he could reach it easily.

"My parents are still trying to work that out. There's some problem with the insurance. I just wish they'd let me wait at home. Sitting here all day is getting to me. Luckily, Michael is coming by after football practice and has promised to spend the rest of the afternoon."

"Michael Valdez?" I confirmed, as Warren dug into his lunch.

"Yeah. We hung out at my dad's camp last summer and became good friends. It's killing me that I won't be able to play in the big game with him and the rest of the guys."

"I'm sure the team misses you," I sympathized. "Did you ever hear anything more about who ran you off the road?"

"Not officially, but the guys are convinced it was Griswold. He has a reputation for doing anything it takes to win. I've never played for him, but Michael did when he was a kid. Say's the guy is bad news."

"Bad news?" I asked.

Warren shoved a handful of fries into his mouth and chewed. "Michael said he was obsessed with winning. His practices were brutal, and if you screwed up, he made you run laps till you dropped. A lot of kids ended up quitting."

"I'm surprised their parents didn't complain."

Warren shrugged. "A few did, but the team was mostly undefeated so most didn't say anything. There's something most parents won't 'fess up to, but the truth is, they like to win."

I talked with Warren a while longer and then returned to the shelter. The least glamorous part of my job is the significant amount of cleaning that's required to keep all the pens and cages sanitized. Jeremy and I usually trade off cleaning the bear cage, and today was my turn. Not a pleasant way to spend the afternoon, but a necessary one all the same.

Other than cleaning it had been a slow afternoon, so I decided to cut out early. I was trying to decide whether to use the time to go kayaking or hit the haunted barn when my phone rang. It was Jeremy, informing me that someone had called to complain about a dog howling at the Henderson place. He had a date and wondered if I'd have time to check it out.

Let me state for the record that I am normally a brave sort who rarely shies away from any act that's required to do my job and do it well. But Hezekiah Henderson was a crazed lunatic in life and has, by all accounts, continued to be just as crazy in death.

"You want me to respond to a call at the Henderson place?" I asked. "Alone?" I cringed. "You know that place is haunted."

"I know. I'd go myself, but Gina really isn't one to be kept waiting."

"I really don't understand why you continue to date her," I found myself saying, even though it was really none of my business.

"Have you seen her?"

I had.

"Okay, I'll go." I looked reluctantly at the darkening sky. "What's the situation exactly?"

"The neighbors to the south called and complained that there's been a dog howling for hours. They think it's trapped inside the house and asked if we could pick it up."

"Okay," I sighed, "I'm on my way."

The Henderson house, under any other circumstances, would most likely be considered a quite normal place. Two-storied with an attic, it sits toward the back of a large, overgrown lot surrounded by an iron fence and an impenetrable gate that opens onto a dirt drive leading to a walkway comprised of four rotted steps and an equally rotted porch.

Hezekiah had been an old man already when I was a child. A *crazy* old man, I'd like to reiterate. Although he seemed to have adequate financial resources to do whatever it was he wanted, what he chose was to live as a recluse who rarely, if ever, left his creepy old house.

When I was seven, one of my classmates told me that, in his youth, Hezekiah had murdered and then dismembered over a hundred people. It was rumored that he buried the body parts under the floorboards in the basement and then settled into a life of seclusion in order to maintain the spell he'd used to trap the souls of his victims in a sort of limbo for all time.

As I turned onto the dirt drive, I reminded myself that the story couldn't possibly be true. If Hezekiah *had* murdered a hundred people, he surely would have been arrested, and even if he'd managed to avoid incarceration due to some powerful black magic, as many of the kids in town believed, the spell would have been broken and the souls released the moment the old man finally died. As with many local legends, no one in town will admit to actually believing the strange tale, but when Hezekiah died and a distant heir tried to sell the property, no one would buy it for any price. As a result the house has stood empty for more than fifteen years.

As I stood before the front gate with Charlie at my side, I listened for voices in the inky night. It's not that I believe in ghosts, exactly, but even the most stalwart nonbeliever would have to admit that in the fifteen years the house has been empty, strange and unexplainable occurrences have taken place within its walls. Hezekiah died when I was nine. For years no one dared enter the creepy structure, but as time went by the rumors ceased, and homeless vagrants began to use the building to ward off cold winter nights. The legend of Hezekiah Henderson and the haunted basement faded and became dormant until I was fifteen and three homeless men were found dead from no apparent cause other than fear-induced heart failure.

When I was seventeen, a group of kids prowling the streets late at night reported hearing the sound of crying from within the dark walls, and when I was twenty, something that looked a lot like blood appeared on the back exterior wall. According to the authorities, these incidents, as well as several others, had logical and scientific explanations, although no one has actually revealed what those explanations might be. Most accept the vague answers they've been given, but there are those of us who wonder if, perhaps, the house really is haunted.

I seriously considered turning around and high-tailing it out of there when I heard the most sorrowful howling. "So what do you think?" I asked Charlie. "Should we brave the spooky house or come back in the morning when it's light?"

Charlie barked once and trotted through the gate someone had left open. He headed down the rutted dirt drive with nary a care in the world. I thought about calling him back but knew I'd never be able to sleep if I didn't rescue the poor dog trapped inside the house. I grabbed a flashlight from my truck, worked up what little courage I possessed, and slowly followed Charlie down the overgrown drive.

"I'm an adult," I reminded myself aloud. "I no longer believe in ghosts. Creatures that exist only in my imagination cannot hurt me."

I stopped walking and looked at the dilapidated old house, which seemed to take on a life of its own the closer I got. I tried to control my imagination as shadows fluttered across cracked windows, and the once stylish shutters hung loosely so as to creak and clatter in the wind. My heart pounded so loudly I could hear it as I stood at the bottom of the five rotted steps leading to the equally rotted front porch. I knew my fear was unfounded, yet I found myself unable to continue on. I pulled my phone out of my pocket and called a familiar number.

"Hey, what's up?" Ellie answered.

"I'm at the Henderson place."

"Why?" Ellie sounded as horrified as I felt.

"There's a dog trapped somewhere inside. I need to go in and see if I can find him, but all those stories we told as kids are repeating themselves in my imagination and I'm totally freaking out."

"Have Jeremy meet you there," Ellie suggested.

"He has a date."

"Okay." Ellie paused. "Then just wait until morning. I'm sure the dog will be fine."

I was seriously considering just that option when the dog began howling again. "I can't wait. The poor thing sounds terrified."

"You can't go in alone," Ellie warned.

"I know. That's why I called you."

"You want *me* to go in with you?"

"Sort of." I could almost see Ellie's look of panic. "I'm going to go in, but I want you to talk to me while I look for the dog. That way if there *is* a deranged serial killer or vengeful spirit inside, you can call the sheriff and tell them where to find my body."

"That's not funny," Ellie scolded.

"I know," I agreed in a slightly more serious tone. "I'm going to start up the steps now. It's dark, so I have the phone in one hand and my flashlight in the other. If I accidently drop the phone while I try to work the lock on the front door, don't panic."

"Okay."

I could hear Ellie breathing in my ear as I carefully made my way up the broken steps and across the rotted porch. I noticed that the front door had been left ajar, saving me the trouble of breaking in. I giggled as I pushed it farther open, and it gave a huge moan, like a bad cliché.

"What was that?" Ellie must have heard the door as well.

"The front door," I answered.

"Are you inside?"

"Yeah," I answered as I stepped inside. I shone my flashlight around the large entry hall and tried to get my bearings.

"What do you see?" Ellie whispered.

"Someone has been here recently. There's fresh graffiti on the walls."

"You don't think they're still there?"

I hoped not.

"Can you tell where the dog is?" Ellie wondered.

I listened as the howling grew louder. "It seems to be coming from the basement."

"The basement?" Ellie gasped. "You can't go into the basement. That's where all the bodies are."

"I'm sure if there really were bodies, someone would have found them by now." I sounded braver than I felt. "I'll just pop down, free the dog, then get the hell out of here."

I stood in the middle of the room and tried to figure out how to access the basement. Through the kitchen? Seemed a logical choice, although I had no idea where the kitchen was. There were stairs in front of me and hallways to both the left and the right. The basement wouldn't be up, which left me a fifty/fifty chance of guessing right the first time.

"Have you ever been in here?" I asked.

"God, no," Ellie said. "Why do you ask?"

"I'm trying to figure out how to get into the basement. The wailing coming from the dog is echoing all around me so I can't tell in which direction to look."

"Are you sure you don't just want to come back in the morning?" Ellie tried again.

Something crashed overhead. My heart leaped into my throat as I stifled a scream.

"Did something fall?" Ellie asked.

I couldn't help but imagine all sorts of undead creatures prowling around upstairs. I focused on slowing my breathing as I struggled to answer. "It was probably just the wind."

I decided to take the hallway to the left. It was dark and narrow. All of the doors were closed. I opened each one as I made my way toward the back of the house. Most of the rooms were bedrooms, covered in dust and cobwebs. There was a small bathroom with something that looked a lot like blood smeared across the front of the sink and onto the floor.

"It looks like there's blood in the bathroom," I breathed as my heart pounded in my chest.

"What?" Ellie gasped. "Get out of there. Call the sheriff to let the dog out. At least he has a gun."

"Guns don't work on ghosts," I reminded her.

"Maybe not, but they work on maniacal serial killers. I really think you should leave."

"Yeah, maybe you're right."

As I exited the bathroom, I noticed that Charlie, who had been walking right next to me as we made our way down the hall, was now sitting in front of a door at the very end. I *really* didn't want to open it, but my sympathy for the poor dog trapped in the dark won out over my fear. Beyond the door was a stairway leading down, I assumed, to the basement.

"I found the stairs to the basement," I told Ellie.

"You aren't going down?"

"I've come this far. Charlie is with me. It'll be fine."

"You know that you're insane?"

"So I've been told." I hesitated for just a minute before carefully making my way down the partially rotted staircase. When I reached the bottom I slowly turned the handle on the rusty doorknob. The door was stuck, most likely rusted with age. I put my shoulder into it, opening it just a crack but enough for a medium-sized black dog to rush through. The dog ran up the stairs and I was just about to make my own hasty escape when Charlie ran into the room the black dog had just vacated.

"Charlie," I whispered. I have no idea why I whispered. It seemed the thing to do in a spooky old house on an inky black night.

Charlie barked but didn't respond to my call.

"What's wrong?" Ellie asked.

"Charlie, come," I demanded in a much sterner tone.

Charlie whined but refused to obey.

"Are you okay?" Ellie sounded panicked.

"Charlie went into the basement," I said. "I'm going to set the phone down while I get him. If I scream, call for help."

I set the phone on the floor by the door. It took both hands and most of my strength to push the door open enough to squeeze through. I shone my flashlight around the musty old room. The first thing I noticed were footprints in the dust and a trail of what looked a lot like blood smeared across the floor. I stifled a scream as I frantically looked for any sign of Charlie.

"This isn't funny," I insisted. "We're in a spooky old house two days before Halloween. If this were a movie, we'd be dead by now. Get your furry butt out here."

Nothing.

I began to walk forward slowly using my flashlight to search the room, where I found Charlie guarding what appeared to be a very dead body.

Chapter 8

After a twenty-minute interrogation by Sheriff Salinger, Charlie and I headed over to our Thursday-night book club meeting at the senior center.

I'm sure you're wondering why I didn't just go home after such a harrowing experience. But the last thing I wanted was to be alone, and Ellie had a date and Levi wasn't answering his cell. Besides, I find the group of seniors I share this particular hobby with to be comforting. Most don't understand why I want to engage in discourse with a group of geriatrics, but suffice it to say that as far as I'm concerned, the depth of knowledge and understanding these golden-agers bring to the table by far supersede any communication issues that might exist due to the generation gap between us.

There are seven human members of the club including myself, and six canine members including Charlie. I settled Charlie with the other dogs in attendance and took a seat between my grandfather, who I refer to as Pappy but others refer to as Luke, and Tanner Brown, a crusty old fisherman who runs charters on the lake.

I'd been instructed by Salinger not to discuss the murder, a directive I realized was going to be close to impossible to obey.

"Are the fish biting?" I politely asked Tanner after kissing Pappy on the cheek. I don't really care if the fish are biting; in fact, I find the whole concept revolting. Still, my dad raised me to be polite, and part of being polite is the making of gracious conversation. Besides, talking about fish would, at least temporarily, help me to keep my promise to our good sheriff.

"Can't complain," Tanner said.

"It looks like Buddy is doing better this week." Buddy is Tanner's sixteen-year-old golden retriever, who has a tendency toward arthritis.

"Yeah, vet gave him some new meds. He seems to be takin' to 'em. He even came out on the boat with me this morning."

"I'm glad to hear it."

I turned toward Pappy and smiled. A few minutes of chitchat are about my limit with Tanner. Not that he isn't a perfectly nice guy, but his inventory of conversational subjects seems limited to fishing, his dog, and something I try at all cost to avoid discussing: deer hunting.

"I found out an interesting piece of information yesterday," I began. "It seems that my mother is in town, and apparently everyone who isn't me has known of her presence for quite some time." There was nothing better to distract me from a murder than discussion of my mother.

Pappy's eyes crinkled in the corners as he shot me an amused look. "Everyone who isn't you?"

"Well, maybe not everyone," I admitted. "But Zak mentioned it, and I know Dad knows. I can't believe he didn't tell me."

"Maybe he didn't want to upset you."

"Why would he think I'd be upset?"

"Are you upset?"

"Of course I'm upset," I screeched a bit too loudly for polite company.

I blushed, and Pappy squeezed my hand in a gesture of support. Perhaps book club wasn't the best venue for this particular conversation.

"Your dad loves you more than anything," Pappy reminded me. "If he didn't tell you, he probably has a really good reason. He'll tell you when he's ready."

"Yeah," I conceded. "I know you're right."

I'd thought several times today about paying my old man a visit and confronting him about his dinner with my mother, but some nagging instinct buried deep down inside had convinced me otherwise. I don't know why my dad hasn't chosen to fill me in on his visit with my mother, but I do know that Pappy was dead on when he stated that my dad loves me. He would never do anything to hurt me, and I know he'll tell me when he's ready.

I turned to watch the dogs play while Phyllis King, a retired English teacher, fussed with tea and cookies. No one really wants the tea and cookies, but Phyllis insists they're a must at any civilized soirée, so every week she brings them and every week we politely consume them.

"Okay, let's go ahead and get started," Hazel Hampton, town librarian and book club leader, announced.

"If I may," Ernie Valdez interrupted the group, "I'd like to make an announcement now that we're all gathered. I guess you all heard about Warren Trent's accident."

Based on the affirmative murmurs in the room, it seemed apparent that everyone had.

"Warren is a good friend of my grandson Michael. I spoke to Warren's father today, and apparently there have been a few complications. The doctor has recommended surgery to head off problems down the road. The procedure is going to require an extended hospital stay, and the Trent family's insurance won't cover the entire cost of the operation. I'd like to propose that our group organize a fund-raiser to help the family with expenses."

"Oh, dear," Phyllis tsk-tsked. "We most certainly should help. Does anyone have any suggestions as to the type of fund-raiser we should sponsor?"

"How about a bake sale?" Hazel suggested.

"Do you have any idea how many cupcakes you'd have to sell to pay for even a small portion of an average hospital bill?" I asked.

"Do you have a better idea?" Hazel countered.

I didn't.

"Maybe we could pass around a donation jar at the community picnic," Nick suggested. "I bet there are a lot of folks who would pitch in to help a neighbor in need."

"That's not a bad idea," I said, trying for a softer approach than the one I'd taken with Hazel. "But what we really need to do is figure out a way to get a larger amount of money from fewer people."

"How about a raffle?" Pappy suggested.

The idea had merit. A raffle would require only a minimal amount of extra work, and we could sell the tickets at all the upcoming community events.

"The Kiwanis made over twenty grand last year when they raffled off that car," Nick pointed out.

"Where are we going to get a car?" Phyllis asked.

"Maybe we could get someone to donate one," Tanner said.

"If someone is willing to donate a twenty-thousand-dollar car, wouldn't it be easier to just ask them to donate the twenty grand?" Phyllis pointed out.

"I think this subject is going to require considerable thought," Hazel observed. "Perhaps we can set up a special committee to come up with a plan."

Based on the echoes of "yeah," and "good idea," in the room, it seemed as though the group agreed.

"Okay, it seems like we have a plan," Hazel said. "If there is nothing else…"

"Someone killed Coach Griswold and dumped his body in the basement of the old Henderson place," I blurted out.

I took a deep sigh as the pressure that had been building up as I tried to keep the secret was finally released.

"What?" was the consensus in the room.

"Charlie and I went out to the house to respond to a call about a howling dog and we found Griswold deader than a doornail on the floor in the basement."

"Oh, my." Hazel put her hand to her chest as if she might be having a heart attack. "Who could have done such a thing?"

I had my suspicions, but for once I kept my mouth shut.

"You don't think this has anything to do with the football nonsense that's been going on?" Phyllis asked after several minutes of stunned silence.

"Oh, I'm sure it can't be." Nick seemed shocked by the suggestion. "Although, coupled with the upcoming holiday, the pranks do seem to have escalated this year. Still I can't believe anyone would kill someone over a football rivalry."

"Stranger things have happened once you get folks all riled up," Tanner warned. "I read a study once on how perfectly nice folks can become violent when acting as part of a group."

"Yes, but we're talking about a football game and not a political demonstration," Nick argued. "Do we know how Coach Griswold died?"

Everyone looked at me. "Sheriff Salinger is still looking into it," I replied.

"Yes, but what did you see, dear?" Hazel wondered.

What I saw will assuredly give me nightmares for years. The man was dressed in blood-soaked clothes and his limbs were arranged in such a way as to indicate that several bones at least were broken, which could be explained by the fact that it appeared as though he had been murdered upstairs and then dragged down to the basement. Someone had tossed an old rag over his head, so at least I didn't have to look at his face. I didn't even know it was Griswold's body I'd found until Sheriff Salinger showed up.

"I didn't see much really." I strained to pull off just the right amount of nonchalance. Salinger had warned me that revealing the details of the murder could compromise his investigation. I didn't want to interfere with the law, but I was itching to tell everyone what I knew. "Charlie and I got out of the room pretty quick once we realized what we'd found."

"It's hard to believe something like this could happen in our little town," Phyllis commented.

"Why *did* it happen in our town?" Pappy said. "Coach Griswold lives in Bryton Lake now. What was he even doing here?"

"Maybe he was killed in Bryton Lake and then transported to the Henderson place by whoever killed him," Nick speculated.

"But why?" Pappy asked. "Why bring his body to Ashton Falls?"

"The house is pretty isolated," Nick pointed out. "And it's been deserted for quite some time."

"He did used to live here," Pappy speculated. "I'm sure he still has friends he comes around to visit. Maybe he was in town when he got himself wacked."

"My money is on Frances Wadsworth," Phyllis speculated. "She dated Griswold, you know. Bastard broke her heart."

"That was five years ago," Pappy reasoned. "Besides, why would Frances lure him to the Henderson place? The whole thing seems sloppy. If Frances had killed him, she would have done it so much more eloquently."

"True," Phyllis acknowledged. Frances was a proper Southern belle who had moved to Ashton Falls after her husband died.

"If I killed someone I'd tie a cement block to them and dump them in the lake," Tanner offered. "Fish would take care of the evidence."

"Not me. I'd use poison," Hazel said. "No fuss, no muss."

"Gunshot through the heart would be more humane," Ernie countered.

"I'd go with a shot of a quick-acting sedative to stop the heart," Nick chimed in.

I could see the discussion was quickly disintegrating and I was tired. It was unlikely that the conversation would get back around to the book we were supposed to be discussing, so I made my excuses and left. I'd already said more than I should have. Salinger was going to kill me. If I was going to spend the next day in jail for obstruction of justice, I'd better get a good night's sleep tonight.

Chapter 9

The phone rang, wakening me from a deep sleep and the most delicious dream I'd had in quite some time.

It was Zak.

"Do you have any idea what time it is?" I groaned. Charlie yawned and readjusted his position on the bed while Spade and Marlow opted for an irritated leap to the floor and an angry scurry out the bedroom door.

"One thirty-eight," he replied.

"Why are you calling me at one thirty-eight?"

"Levi is in jail. They arrested him for the murder of Coach Griswold."

"What?" I bolted upright. I turned on the bedside light and looked around the room. I figured I had to be dreaming. That made about as much sense as anything. Why in the world would anyone think Levi killed Coach Griswold?

I must have voiced my thought out loud because Zak responded. "Levi was seen arguing with Griswold Wednesday afternoon. It's been determined that the time of death was some time Wednesday night."

"Seems like a pretty weak reason to arrest a guy," I pointed out.

"In and of itself, yes, but Levi also happens to be in possession of the letterhead someone used to blackmail Griswold."

I paused to rub my eyes. "Someone was blackmailing Griswold?" I asked.

I heard Zak take a deep breath. "Sorry, I guess I'm getting a little ahead of myself. Perhaps I should start at the beginning."

"Have you called Ellie?" I asked.

"No, I figured I'd call you first."

"Okay." My brain was finally beginning to work. "I'll call Ellie and fill her in. Then I'll put on some coffee. Why don't you come over and bring us both up to date?"

"I'm sitting in my car in front of the sheriff's office," Zak informed me. "I'll be there in ten minutes."

Ten minutes wasn't a lot of time, but I somehow managed to start the coffee, get dressed, brush my teeth, and call Ellie. By the time Zak arrived I felt and looked almost human. And by the time Ellie arrived we had heated the pastries Zak thought to pick up at the all-night market. Once we'd poured our coffee and selected our pastries, we sat down at the kitchen table and waited for Zak to fill us in on the nightmare we'd stumbled into.

"After Griswold's body was found, Salinger asked Levi to come in and answer some questions," Zak began. "Levi cooperated. Salinger conducted the interview and then announced that they planned to keep him in custody for the time being. I guess he tried to call you," he looked at me, "but you didn't answer, and then he called Ellie, only to find out she was out on a date. In the end he got hold of me, and I went down to the station."

"I can't believe Levi didn't tell me what was going on when he called," Ellie complained. "I was out with Rick, but he has to know that I would have dumped Rick and come running had I known what was going on."

"I don't think he wanted you to have to cancel your date," Zak responded.

"Not cancel my date?" Ellie shrieked. "Is he insane? He's been arrested for *murder*," she emphasized. "Of course I would have canceled my date."

"Don't feel bad," I tried to console her. "I didn't even answer the phone when he called."

Ellie gave me the oddest look.

"Book club," I explained.

"I feel just awful." Tears began streaming down Ellie's cheeks. "I should have realized something was wrong, but he sounded so normal on the phone. He asked if I was busy, and I told him I was out with Rick. He said it was no big deal, that we'd catch up tomorrow, and then he hung up."

"Look, we both feel bad that we weren't there for Levi when he needed us, but we can be there for him now," I pointed out. "How could Salinger think Levi would do something like this?"

"It turns out that Griswold was accused of breaking a kid's arm when he coached kiddie league here in Ashton Falls," Zak began. "Apparently the kid, whose name is Ryan Tillman, used to play for Levi but has since graduated. Somehow during a conversation, Ryan mentioned it to Levi. To make matters worse, he told Levi he wasn't the only one Griswold used to kick around. Levi was furious, so he went to Bryton Lake and confronted Griswold. The argument ended in a fist fight. The police at Bryton Lake were called by a neighbor, but neither man wanted to press charges, so they let Levi leave. I guess this happened just hours before Griswold was murdered."

I thought about the mascot at Bryton Lake Academy. He'd seemed terrified about what Griswold would do if he didn't retrieve the beaver costume.

"How did he die?" Ellie asked.

"Someone hit him over the head with something cylindrical, probably a bat," Levi supplied. "Salinger figures that Levi left when ordered to by the police but then either he returned or Griswold followed him to Ashton Falls. Either way, Griswold is dead and Levi is their prime suspect."

Ellie looked like she was going to pass out.

"You mentioned a blackmail letter?" I urged.

"Salinger found a file in Griswold's office at Bryton Lake Academy. It contained copies of a letter addressed to Griswold. The letter simply said, 'I saw what you did,' followed by instructions outlining how much money was required and where to deliver it. The letter is on Ashton Falls Events Committee letterhead."

Ellie interjected, "There are nine people on the committee including Zoe and me."

"Levi is the only one with a motive," Zak reminded her.

"That we know of," I pointed out. "Besides, it sounds like Levi heard about the abuse and immediately went to Bryton Lake to confront Griswold. When did he have time to write and deliver a blackmail note?"

"Good point." Zak smiled. "I'll mention that to the attorney I hired. Salinger is refusing to release Levi, so there's not much we can do until court opens in the morning, but the guy I hired to defend Levi is the best there is. I'm certain he can get him released based on the fact that all Salinger has at this point is a theory. That doesn't mean Salinger won't keep looking for something more concrete, though. He seemed pretty convinced Levi is guilty."

"So what now?" Ellie wondered. "How do we help Levi?"

"We have to find out what really happened," I said. "If we can find the real killer, we can clear Levi's name."

"You know Salinger is going to have a fit if you start nosing around in this," Ellie warned her. "The last time you got in the middle of a police investigation, Salinger threatened to have you fired from your job."

"That was different," I argued. "The last time I was just trying to do my job. Can I help it if Salinger's drug dealer was also abusing his dog? Besides, this is Levi. We *have* to help."

"Maybe we should all get some sleep and revisit this in the morning. What does everyone's schedule look like?"

"I'm supposed to work, but Jeremy can cover for me."

"I can get away, too," Ellie said. "Someone can cover for me at the diner."

"Okay, then, let's meet in the morning and figure out a plan," Zak suggested. "We can meet here. I'll bring breakfast. Say nine o'clock? That will give me a chance to make sure Levi is released."

"I'll be here," I confirmed.

"Me, too," Ellie added.

Chapter 10

I was never so glad to see anyone as I was to see Levi walk through my front door with Zak later that morning. He looked exhausted, although I doubted he was any more tired than I was, considering I'd never gotten back to sleep after Zak and Ellie left. The up side to insomnia was that my boathouse was cleaner than it had been for a very long time. After everyone hugged everyone else, we settled in to eat the breakfast sandwiches Zak had brought with him.

"So they let you go on your own recognizance?" I confirmed with Levi.

"The attorney Zak hired for me convinced the judge that the only evidence they have against me is circumstantial at best. I've been warned not to leave the area, but basically I'm free to go about my business as usual."

"The game," I realized.

"Lamé got a sub for my classes, but he's agreed to let me attend the pep rally and game as planned." Levi looked at his watch. "I really should get home to shower and change. The pep rally is at eleven. You'll be there?" He looked at Ellie and me.

"I wouldn't miss it," I assured him.

"Me neither." Ellie smiled. "I really should stop off at Rosie's first, though, to make sure everything is covered. I can give you a ride home," she offered Levi.

"I'd appreciate that." Levi stood up and hugged Zak and me. He thanked us both again and left with

Ellie, who had arranged to meet me at the high school gymnasium at ten forty-five.

"Do you think he's in the clear?" I asked Zak when we were alone.

"Not really," he replied. "The sheriff doesn't have enough evidence to hold him at this point, but that doesn't mean he won't keep looking. Salinger has as much as said that he still considers Levi to be his prime suspect."

"Did you bring up the fact that Levi didn't even find out about the abuse until after the blackmail letter was sent?" I asked as I began to load the dishwasher. Charlie and Lambda were lying in the sun on the deck just outside the kitchen window. Normally the view beyond my boathouse soothes my soul on even the stormiest of days, but today I found little solace in the serenity of my lakeside home.

"Yeah, but Salinger pointed out that we can't prove *when* Levi became aware of the situation. He could have found out, sent the letter, and then waited to confront Griswold when he wouldn't pay up." Zak took a dishrag from the drawer and began wiping down the kitchen table.

"That's nuts. All they have to do is talk to Ryan."

"I agree, but Levi is an easy target and Salinger is looking for easy."

"Do we know if Griswold ever paid the blackmailer any money?"

"I assume the sheriff is looking into it, but at this point he refuses to talk about it. I could probably hack into his bank records, but I'm not sure that's the wisest thing to do at this point."

"Yeah, I'm sure Salinger will be keeping an eye on all of us with Levi being his prime suspect." I poured myself a cup of coffee and topped off the one Zak had been drinking. "Still, I suppose trying to track down the person behind the blackmail is a good idea. You mentioned that the letter Griswold received was on Ashton Falls Event Committee letterhead. As Ellie said, there are nine people on the committee, but I can't imagine any of them being responsible for Griswold's death."

"Do any of them have kids who might have played football for Griswold at some point?" Zak asked. "Maybe if we can narrow down who might have a motive, it will point us in the right direction."

I thought about it. "Ellie, Levi, and I are all on the committee. None of us have kids, but I guess if we're looking at things in a totally unbiased way, we'd have to have Levi on the list; it's well known that he cares deeply for the kids he coaches and would feel protective toward them."

"Do you have a pad of paper?" Zak asked.

"Top drawer next to the phone."

Zak retrieved the pad and wrote down my name, as well as Ellie's and Levi's. He put a star next to Levi's name. "I think we should look at not only committee members but those with proximity to committee members who might have access to the letterhead."

"Like family members or employees?"

"Exactly."

I systematically worked through the committee members in my mind. "Willa Walton has a son, Jeremiah, who used to play football, but he graduated two years ago so I doubt she'd try to get revenge at this point. Frank Valdez has a son currently on Levi's team. He's a senior now, but Warren mentioned to me that Michael played kiddie league with Griswold before he left the area to serve as coach for Bryton Lake. Still, I can't see Frank killing anyone."

Zak added Frank and Willa to the list.

I thought about the other members of the committee. Although Hazel Hampton didn't have children of her own, as the town librarian she was known and loved by many of the kids, Like Frank and Levi, I couldn't imagine she could hurt a fly, but I suggested to Zak that we add her.

My dad, Hank Donovan, was on the committee and had only one child, me, who didn't play football, though Gary Quinby, who had worked at Donovan's all through high school, had played for Griswold. Gary was in New York attending college, so it seemed unlikely he was behind the blackmail, and there was no way my dad would hurt anyone, although he did tend to be overprotective of those he loved.

It almost killed me to do it, but I added his name to the list.

"What about Tawny?" Zak asked. "She runs the preschool. I'm sure some of her kids must grow up to play football."

"No," I disagreed, "the timing is wrong. Tawny started the preschool five years ago. None of her kids would have been old enough to play football when Griswold   coached the kiddie league and none are in high school yet, so they wouldn't play for him now. Gilda Reynolds' theater arts program might have some kids that overlap, though."

Zak added her to the list.

"Are you wearing a costume to the pep rally?" I changed the subject. I wanted to find Griswold's killer and clear Levi, but our current exercise seemed futile at best. Neither of us really believed that anyone from the committee had killed Griswold. I suppose making the list made us feel like we were doing *something*, but in the end I knew that Griswold's killer wouldn't be found among the town's most dedicated volunteers.

"I have a mask I wore a few years ago. I figured I'd slip it on," Zak said. "You?"

"To be honest, I haven't had a chance to give it much thought. I'm supposed to meet Ellie in a half hour, so I won't have time to come up with much."

"We'll stop by my place on the way. I have several masks from years past. You can borrow one."

The high school gymnasium was packed to capacity with fans gathered to celebrate their team. Hazel must have gotten the word out about the costumes; a good two-thirds of those in attendance had on a mask or costume of one type or another. "The place is packed," I commented as Zak and I squeezed in next to Ellie on a wooden bench of the gymnasium bleachers. Levi was busy with the team, so I doubted we'd see him again until after the game.

"*Planet of the Apes*?" Ellie asked as she considered my mask.

"Planet of the I didn't have a costume and Zak had this on hand," I replied. "I like your costume. Those shorts are like, wow, but I have to say you make a pretty believable Daisy Duke."

"Thanks."

Zak, who was sitting to my left, was speaking to Nick Benson, on his other side and wearing a Frankenstein head, a torn white lab coat left over from the forty years he'd practiced medicine in Ashton Falls, and sturdy boots.

"I'm not sure I like the cheerleaders' new uniforms," Ellie said as the ten girls who made up the spirit squad marched onto the stage. "They seem too dark."

The old uniforms had been gold with accents of black, while the new uniforms were black with only the school letters in gold. Personally, I like the black, but Ellie is known for her love of all things bright and flashy.

The gym vibrated with enthusiasm as the girls began the routine they must have spent hours perfecting. It was good to be part of such a large body of positive energy after the stress of the past twenty-four hours. There had been some speculation that the game would be canceled with the news of Coach Griswold's death, but the administration at Bryton Lake Academy had decided it was best to play the game as scheduled with the assistant coach filling in.

The noise in the gym was overwhelming as fans clapped their hands, stomped their feet, and shouted along with the girls leading the cheers. It was getting hot, so I took off my ape head and set it on the bench beside me.

"Here comes Levi." Ellie grabbed my arm in excitement as Levi made his way to the stage to introduce the team. "Doesn't he look handsome?"

I turned to look at Ellie, who suddenly seemed like a teenager in love. Levi and Ellie? I'd never stopped to consider the fact that I might be the third wheel in our trio. I always figured if there was going to be a pairing off, it would be Levi and me. Of course, I'd rejected that idea years ago.

I watched Ellie as she cheered for each member of the team as his name was announced. Her eyes glowed, her cheeks were flushed, and her smile seemed to light up the already bright gym. There was no doubt about it: Ellie was in love and, based on the way her attention was glued to Levi, I couldn't deny who she was jonesing for. I wasn't sure how I felt about that. On one hand, I loved both Levi and Ellie and wanted them to be happy, but on the other, a romance between the two would definitely alter the dynamic that had served us well for most of our lives.

"You know," Ellie leaned toward me so that I could hear her over the roar in the room, "as much as I don't like the cheerleaders' new uniforms, I really love the new jerseys the guys got. Levi looks really good in black, don't you think?"

"Black is a good color for him," I said.

I diverted my attention from Ellie's happy smile to Levi's somewhat more forced one as he presented an obviously rehearsed speech. I couldn't help but wonder if Levi was crushing on Ellie the way she seemed to be crushing on him. Neither had said anything about a change in their relationship status, and I had to believe that if the pair acted on their newfound feelings they would say something. Wouldn't they?

"What's with the frown?" Zak put his freakishly large arm around my shoulder.

"Just thinking about the murder," I lied.

"Not much we can do about it at this point, so you may as well relax and enjoy the show."

"Has Levi said anything to you about having a new girlfriend?" I found myself asking almost against my will.

"Girlfriend? Why, you crushing on him?"

I rolled my eyes. "Of course not. It's just…" I hesitated. "Never mind."

"I think he was going out with the new physical education teacher at the high school, but I seem to remember him saying they broke up."

"Yeah," I acknowledged. "That's been over for a while."

One of the cheerleaders fell from the human pyramid and everyone in the gym groaned.

"It looks like the rally is about over," Ellie stated. "I told Levi we'd meet up afterward and grab lunch. He'll be tied up the rest of the afternoon with prep for the game."

"You guys go ahead. I really should stop by to check in at the shelter. I'll meet you there."

"Want me to order for you?" Ellie offered.

"Veggie sandwich on whole wheat," I answered. "Oh and apple crisp for dessert if Rosie has any today. I won't be long."

Chapter 11

I didn't really need to stop in at the shelter; Jeremy was quite capable of handling whatever might come up in my absence. I just used the visit as an excuse to put a little distance between Ellie and me while I figured out what I was going to do about the whole Levi situation. I'd known Ellie for long enough to recognize when she was hooked on someone, and if I was reading things correctly, her feelings toward Levi had migrated from friendship toward something more.

"I'm glad you're here," Jeremy greeted me the minute I walked through the door.

I bent down as Charlie trotted over to say hello. Most times I took Charlie with me wherever I went, but I figured the noise and intensity of the rally would be too much for the little guy.

"Bryton Lake called and asked if we could take four more dogs. They said they'd deliver them if need be. Someone brought in ten rescues and they're booked beyond capacity."

"Bryton Lake is always booked to capacity. Don't they ever recruit people to adopt their dogs?" I sounded bitchy and I knew it. I know the folks at the Bryton Lake shelter do the best they can with what they have to work with.

"Does that mean no?" Jeremy sounded uncertain.

"No, of course we'll take the dogs. I'm sorry; I guess this murder thing is getting to me."

The truth of the matter was, it was less the murder and more the Levi and Ellie thing that had my knickers in a knot, but I wasn't going to admit that to Jeremy. "How many dogs do we currently have on-site?"

"Eight. I arranged for three adoptions this morning."

We had the capacity for more than twenty. "Okay, tell Bryton Lake we'll take eight dogs. That'll give them a little leeway if they have any other dogs come in over the weekend. We could use a few more for the pet adoption booth at the picnic anyway. By the way, did we put an ad in the paper?"

"I dropped it off yesterday. A copy of the proof is on your desk."

"How are our lumberyard mama and kittens doing?"

"Good." Jeremy smiled. "They seem to have settled right in. I already have a waiting list for the babies once they're old enough for homes. I thought I'd talk to Willa about the mama cat if no one claims her. I put her photo in the lost-and-found section of the paper this morning."

"Did you get a chance to put a poster on the billboard in the park?"

"Not yet. I planned to do it as soon as I got a chance."

"I'll take care of it," I offered. "I'm supposed to meet Ellie and Levi for lunch, so I can do it on the way. I'm not sure if I'll be back before the game. Call me if you need me."

"Your cell on?" Jeremy teased. He knew I was famous for leaving it off.

"Yeah, it's on."

"You taking Charlie?"

"Yeah, I'll take him with me. See you at the game?"

"Count on it."

By the time I met up with the others, our food had been delivered and the gang was enthralled in a conversation regarding defensive strategy against the high-scoring Beavers. I settled Charlie under the table before sitting down next to Zak. On any other day I wouldn't have welcomed Zak's presence, but today I found myself thrilled that he was in attendance, saving me from feeling like a third wheel. I realized that I was going to have to figure out a way to deal with the Levi and Ellie situation if I was going to maintain a friendship with two of the most important people in my life, but first I had to figure out if whether either of them even realized there was a situation to figure out.

"I'm telling you," Zak was saying as I sat down next to him, "the Beavers have two guys who can carry the ball. Immobilize them and you immobilize the whole team."

"That may be, but those two guys are averaging two TDs a piece per game," Levi countered. "Short of an injury to one or both, I think the only way we're going to beat the Beavers is to outscore them. Luckily, their defense is worse than ours."

"Everything okay at the shelter?" Zak asked as I bit into my sandwich. "You were gone longer than we expected."

"Bryton Lake is sending over some more dogs. I had to get the details worked out."

"Didn't you pick dogs up from them yesterday?" Levi asked.

"Yeah, but they just received a delivery of rescue dogs and needed more room."

"I heard they busted a guy for running a puppy mill in the area," Ellie added. "Hazel told me that some guy had twenty dogs locked up in cages so small they could barely walk around, The poor things were so emaciated you could see their ribs. When I think of what the poor dogs must have gone through, I get so mad."

I pushed my sandwich aside. If I didn't feel bad before concerning my outburst over the extra dogs, I certainly did now. I told Jeremy we'd take eight dogs, but we had room for more. Maybe I'd call him back and see if I could find out if any of the puppy mill dogs were taken to other shelters in the area. Ellie said there were twenty dogs and Bryton Lake was set to receive ten. I wondered where the other half had gone.

"Zoe, I'm glad I ran into you," Ernie Young from the market greeted me. "I have the items you requested for the kiddie carnival in my van. I was going to drop them off at the shelter, but it looks like you aren't in."

I smiled at Ernie's attempt at humor. "You can leave everything with Jeremy. Were you able to get the bean bags for the tic-tac-toe game?"

"I got them, and some extra-large balloons as well. My toy supplier happened to come by as I was ordering the prizes we talked about, and he donated six boxes of stuffed animals."

"Wow, really. That's awesome," I replied.

"Did you ever find enough zombies for the run?" Ernie asked.

The zombie run. In all the death and mayhem, I had totally forgotten about the zombies. I groaned and buried my face in my hands. There was no way I was going to find enough recruits by tomorrow morning.

"Zak rounded up some guys," Levi said. "I meant to tell you, but with everything else going on… You should have around twenty, and most of them have done it before. I told them to be at Coopers Field by seven."

I flashed both men a look of sincere gratitude. "Thank you. You saved me big time."

"Happy to help." Zak smiled.

If Zak wasn't careful, I was going to stop resenting him and start liking him, a circumstance I figured would be strange and unfamiliar to both of us. As I looked around the table, I realized that, as big a fan as I am of a smooth and consistent equilibrium, that particular state was most likely a thing of the past.

"I should get going," Levi interrupted my ruminations. "I still have a lot to do to get ready for the game. Should we meet up after?"

"Everyone can come over to the boathouse, if you want," I offered. "We can make a fire in the pit and have a few cocktails."

"Sounds good." Levi kissed me on the cheek. "See you then."

"Good luck," I called after him.

"Yeah, break a leg," Ellie said.

"I don't think you're supposed to say that before a football game." Zak laughed. "Would the two of you like a ride to the game? We can leave the extra cars at Zoe's."

"Sounds good to me." Ellie grinned. "I need to make a few stops before the game," I announced. "How about we meet at my place at four? That way we can get to the game early and get good seats."

As Charlie and I drove toward the shelter so that I could check on the whereabouts of the other ten rescue dogs, I thought about how important it was to have good friends. I knew that whatever happened, Levi, Ellie, and even Zak would be there to share my ups and downs, my triumphs and my failures. Yes, things were changing, but I only needed to change with them and a new equilibrium could be found.

Chapter 12

"Who's this?" Ellie asked as she walked in the door of the boathouse several hours later.

"Maggie," I answered. "She's one of the rescue dogs and very pregnant. I couldn't just leave her at the shelter to have her puppies, so I brought her home."

"Uh-oh." Ellie grinned. "Seems like the last time you brought an animal home from the shelter he was here to stay."

Ellie wasn't wrong, Marlow and Spade had both been shelter cats who had come for a visit and stayed. Besides, I was already a little in love with Maggie, a purebred Australian shepherd with black and tan markings and a white chest. In spite of the fact that she had endured intolerable living circumstances for who knew how long, she was surprisingly sweet and gentle.

Ellie knelt down to pet her, and Maggie licked her face. She gently set a paw on her lap, as if to communicate her appreciation for the small amount of attention she was being granted. Her timid disposition made me want to cry. Poor little thing. I just hoped she had enough strength to deliver her pups when the time came.

"She's so skinny," Ellie commented.

"I know. I'm worried about the pups. I had Scott give her a physical before I brought her home. She's been through a lot: beatings, starvation, filthy living conditions. Scott gave me a high-calorie, nutrition-dense dog food to give her, as well as a whole suitcase full of supplements. He doesn't think she's as far along as she looks. We're hoping she'll have time to gain some weight before she delivers."

"Are the other rescues in this bad shape?"

"They aren't in good shape," I admitted.

"I've been thinking about getting a dog."

"Come by the shelter and take a look. I have to warn you, though, that most of the rescues are going to need a gentle hand."

"Are they aggressive?"

"There are two dogs I'm worried about. We're going to keep them at the shelter for a month at least so we can evaluate them before we adopt them out. The other dogs are more skittish than they are aggressive."

When I arrived at the football field I realized that the pregame hijinks that had gripped our town for the past week had changed to Halloween hijinks. Not only was almost every spectator from our team decked out in costume but the goalposts had been wrapped in orange and black crepe paper, a stunt that earned Levi a warning from the head referee and delayed the start of the game by twenty minutes while they were unwrapped.

The cheerleaders had ditched their new uniforms to dress up as sexy vampires, and the team's mascot, Popeye the Bulldog, was wearing a devil cape and horns. "Monster Mash" blasted from the stadium speakers as we waited for the game to begin.

"You people really like your holidays," A woman I recognized as being one of the teachers from Bryton Lake Academy, said as she sat down next to Zak.

As totally strange as this may sound, I actually felt a little jealous when Zak introduced himself and started up a conversation with the very voluptuous educator. I hate to admit it, but Zak is a handsome man. Add that to the fact that he has a ridiculous amount of money and that makes him one of the most eligible bachelors in the entire state. I guess I shouldn't be surprised that the woman was coming on to Zak the way she was. Just because I've never considered him to be date material doesn't mean everyone else with a double X chromosome looks at him in precisely that way.

I tried to focus on what was happening down on the field, but I had to actually stifle a gag when I overheard the woman say that she had a few tricks up her sleeve if Zak was up for a treat. Seriously? Wasn't she a little old for trick-or-treat?

"Something wrong?" Ellie asked. "You were scowling."

"I wasn't scowling," I countered.

Ellie raised an eyebrow, silently challenging me to defend my position.

"Okay, maybe I *was* scowling. The conversation to my left is so syrupy nauseating that I'm having a hard time keeping down my lunch."

Ellie leaned forward so she could look around me. She noticed the woman talking to Zak and smiled.

"What's that for?" I challenged.

"What's what for?" she asked innocently.

"That smile."

"I can't smile?" Her grin broadened.

"Not when the smile means something that totally isn't true," I reasoned.

"Sometimes a smile is just a smile." Ellie's entire face lit up.

I turned to look at Zak, who was whispering something in the woman's ear that made her blush.

"I'm not jealous," I whispered.

"I never said you were." Ellie tried to hide her grin.

"I don't even like Zak."

"I know."

"It's just that it's rude to carry on so…so…" I was rarely ever lost for words, so this was a new experience for me.

"There's Levi." Ellie drew my attention back to the field as Levi and the rest of the coaching staff jogged onto the field. The band started playing the school fight song as the team ran onto the field behind them. As the guys settled in to perform warm-ups, Levi tossed a pumpkin toward the center, who playfully hiked it to the quarterback. I was glad to see that playful Levi had showed up for the game. After all he'd been through, serious and cranky Levi could have been here just as easily.

"Isn't he great?" Ellie gushed.

"Freakin' wonderful." Oops jealous Zoe was back.

Ellie frowned at me.

"I'm just kidding." I tried for the happiest, most carefree voice I could muster. Apparently I was a real bitch when change that I couldn't control came knocking at my door. "You know I love Levi. Leave it to him to bring his funny side to the game in spite of everything that's happened. It's no wonder the kids love him so much."

I couldn't help but smile as Levi chased Popeye around the field as the team filed toward the sideline to allow the opposing team a few minutes of warm-up. The fact that his entire team was cracking up was awesome, but the look of horror on the opposing coach's stuffy, prep-school face was priceless.

"Look, there's Samantha Collins." I pointed her out among the opposing players.

"I thought she was crazy for wanting to play on the team, but her involvement sure has gotten her a lot of attention. I bet she's the most popular girl at her school," Ellie speculated.

"Or the most unpopular," I countered. "Sometimes being a trendsetter isn't all it's cracked up to be."

"Yeah, I guess. Oh good, they're starting."

Even though the Bulldogs' star player was in the hospital, the guys held their own and the game ended with a score of Beavers 24–Bulldogs 21. It was a close game that had me on the edge of my seat the entire time. I felt bad that our team lost, but the guys seemed to be taking the loss in stride in spite of the fact that it was most likely the biggest game of their high school career. Levi was smiling as he jogged with his team to the locker-room, and I hoped he was taking the defeat as well as he seemed to be.

"Poor Levi." Ellie sighed as we walked toward the parking lot.

"I don't know; he seemed okay to me."

"Yeah, I guess he did."

"Levi isn't one to take things too seriously," Zak commented. "He knows how to focus and work hard when it's important to do so, but he also knows how to let go and relax when the situation calls for it."

"Do you think we should wait for Levi?" Ellie asked as we arrived at the parking lot.

"I really should get home to check on Maggie," I said. "I'm sure he'll be along as soon as he finishes with the team."

"Yeah, you're right." Ellie climbed into the backseat of Zak's truck although she was obviously disappointed to be leaving without Levi.

It was a beautiful night. The air was calm, the sky clear, and a million bright stars blanketed the night sky. The four of us sat around the fire Zak had built, sipping on some secret recipe that tasted a lot like pure alcohol. I closed my eyes and listened to the waves from the nearby lake lap gently onto the shore. It was moments like these, when I was comfortable in my corner of the world with my friends and my animals, that I felt the peaceful serenity of the forest surrounding me.

A lone coyote howled in the distance as Ellie laughed at something Levi said. Charlie and Maggie slept at my feet, while Lambda slept behind us. Normally Charlie would be hanging with Lambda, but Maggie was feeling insecure and therefore was glued to my side, and I suspected Charlie's loyalty to me had more to do with jealousy than anything else. Technically I'd only agreed to keep Maggie until she'd weaned her pups, but deep in my heart I knew Ellie was right: Charlie and I had a new housemate.

"Are you sleeping?" Zak asked.

"Um," I replied.

"You're missing an awesome meteor shower."

I opened my eyes as streams of light shot through the sky. "Did you like the house?" I asked. I'm not sure why the fact that Zak had planned to take a look at my grandfather's house popped into my head at that exact moment. I suppose when you let your brain relax for a moment it remembers all the stuff you hadn't even realized you'd forgotten.

"I did," he said. "There are things I'd like to change if I buy it, but the location is fantastic and the basic floor plan acceptable."

"So you're going to buy it?"

"I might." Zak paused. "How would you feel about it if I do?"

Good question. I found that having Zak around wasn't nearly as astringent as it once was. I wouldn't say that under normal circumstances I'd seek out his company, but I realized that I no longer wanted to gouge his eyes out when I saw him. I figure I must be mellowing in my old age.

"I guess it would be okay."

"Then I guess I'll have a conversation with your grandfather."

I smiled a tiny little smile that wouldn't be noticed. I would never admit it to anyone, but I found I was glad Zak would be my new neighbor. I loved my secluded little cove, but having someone just around the bend wouldn't be all that bad. The fact that it was Zak should have horrified me, but somehow it didn't. Maybe change wasn't so bad after all.

Chapter 13

The next morning I realized I shouldn't have worried about not having any zombies for the run; sleep deprivation had apparently turned me into a zombie myself, hoping for a juicy brain to fuel my empty soul. The only saving grace to an impossible situation was that an angel of mercy had shown up even earlier than me and had set everything up, including the registration table, time clock, and finish line. I leaned against a post and closed my eyes. For the first time in my life I really understood how someone could sleep standing up.

"Morning," a voice penetrated the mist that exists between sleep and wakefulness.

I opened my eyes to Zak's smiling face and a large cup of coffee. "You're my angel?"

Zak laughed. "If you'd like."

"You did all this?"

"I got here a little early and decided to get started."

I frowned. "You aren't on drugs, are you?"

Zak looked shocked by the question. "Why would you think that?"

"Because you were up at least as late as I was last night, apparently got up even earlier than I did this morning, and got even less sleep than I did the previous night. I fccl like death warmed over and you look like you're ready to enter this damn run."

Zak shrugged. "I travel a lot. I'm used to getting by on minimal sleep. The guys I lined up should be here any minute. What else do we need to do?"

I looked around and smiled. "Nothing. Absolutely, gloriously nothing."

"Fantastic." Zak led me over to a chair. "You drink your coffee and I'll start signing people in."

In that moment I both loved and hated Zak. I hated him for once again bettering me by showing up all bright eyed and organized at six o'clock in the freaking morning, and I loved him for showing up all bright eyed and organized at six o'clock in the freaking morning. Did I mention that I often have irrational and complicated emotions?

"Wow, everything looks fantastic," Ellie commented two hours later. I was actually surprised that she showed up after the marathon of sleeplessness we'd all endured the past few days. "I ran into a couple of the zombies on my way over and got literal goose bumps."

"Yeah, Zak did a good job making everyone look both dead and deranged," I agreed. "Where's Levi?"

"Having another interview with the sheriff." Ellie sighed. "Salinger is sure Levi is his guy and has been fabricating evidence to prove it."

"Fabricating evidence?" I asked.

"What else could it be? We know Levi would never do something like this, yet Salinger is insisting that Levi had means, motive, and opportunity. When I talked to Levi this morning he seemed really worried."

"Poor Levi," I sympathized. "I hope this gets cleared up soon."

"Yeah, me, too," Ellie agreed. "Where's Charlie?"

"Somewhere with Zak and Lambda. Headed over to the chili cook-off?" I asked.

"Of course." Ellie was a chef by birthright and enjoyed a cooking competition even if it was chili in a park setting. "By the way, I don't know if I should mention this, but I ran into your mother."

"My mother?"

"I stopped off to get a cup of coffee for the road and she was on her way out. I guess she's headed off the mountain to catch a plane for Paris. She said to say hi and she'd catch up with you the next time she was in town."

I found myself wishing Ellie hadn't said anything. My mother can ruin a perfectly wonderful day, even when she isn't around. I don't know why I should let it bother me so much after all these years. She'd never been a real mother to me, and I know in my heart she never will. Still, there'll always be a part of me that *wants* her to want me, the way the little girl inside me had always longed for her.

"I figured the news would upset you and considered not mentioning it at all, but then I realized that I wasn't the only one to see her, and I didn't want you to think I was keeping things from you."

"It's okay." I shrugged. "My mom lost the ability to hurt me a long time ago," I lied. "I figure Ashton Falls is better off without her. Maybe now that my grandfather is selling the house, she'll stay gone for good this time."

My heart sank as I realized that this very well might be true.

"Yeah, maybe." Ellie hugged me. If there's one thing you can say for Ellie, it's that she gives good hugs. The long and hard kind that let you know she feels your pain and wishes to share her comfort. I hugged her back as I fought the tears I knew were waiting just under my barrier of steely self-control.

"On the bright side, I brought you a coffee." She reached into a bag she'd set on the table near me when she first walked up.

"Thanks." I managed a smile.

"So how's the race going?" Ellie asked.

"The lead runners should be coming around that corner any minute." I pointed to the finish line in the distance. "We ended up with some pretty awesome zombies this year. It's going to be hard for the competitors to make it out alive."

"Oh, look, here they come now."

Ellie began clapping and cheering while I prepared to record the runners in order of appearance.

"Isn't that Ryan Tillman?" Ellie asked.

I looked toward a muddy runner in a black shirt. "Yeah, that's him."

"When I talked to Levi, he mentioned that Ryan's statement was one of the main things that kept him on the top of the suspect list. I can't imagine what he could have said that would implicate Levi."

"Let's ask him," I suggested. I had plenty of volunteers to help sort through who was dead and who was alive and who crossed the finish line in what order, so I headed to the snack tent, where Ryan was chatting with a group of guys around his age.

"Ryan," I greeted. "Can I talk to you for a minute? Alone?"

"Yeah, okay." He followed Ellie and me to a shady spot away from the crowd. "What's up?"

"We wanted to ask about your interview with Sheriff Salinger," I began.

Ryan hesitated. "He told me I wasn't supposed to talk about it."

"I realize that." I tried again, "It's just that the sheriff seems to have interpreted something you said as evidence of Coach Denton's guilt in Coach Griswold's death."

Ryan frowned as he tried to work out whether or not to talk to us. "I guess it wouldn't hurt to tell you what I said," he decided. "I ran into Coach Denton a few days ago, and we got to talking about the game. I'm not sure how it came up, but I mentioned that I played on Griswold's team when he coached kiddie league. Coach Denton said something about Coach Griswold demanding the best from his players, and I made a comment about getting kicked around if you didn't give it your all."

"And Coach Denton's response?" I could picture Levi literally exploding. I knew he'd confronted Griswold shortly after talking to Ryan.

"He was pretty mad. He said that people like that shouldn't be allowed to work with kids."

"Did Griswold actually hit you?"

"No," Ryan admitted. "He usually picked the weakest, littlest guy on the team and focused all his negative attention on him. I shot up quite a bit in high school, but I was a skinny runt when I was in kiddie league. He didn't think I should be on the team. He said I was holding them back because league rules required that everyone who was signed up be allowed to play. He tried to get me to quit, but I refused. It totally pissed the guy off. He was always on my case, and if I screwed up, he made me do extra laps. I felt like he intentionally put me in positions where the likelihood of my being injured was greatly increased."

"Why didn't you tell anyone?" I wondered.

"My dad would have killed him if he'd found out. He has a really bad temper that he can't always control. I didn't want him to get in trouble for beating the guy up. Besides," Ryan said with a shrug, "I was used to being kicked around. It was no big deal."

I thought of what he'd said about his dad's inability to control his temper.

"Can you think of anything else you might have said or Salinger might have heard that would cast suspicion on Levi?" Ellie asked.

"Coach Denton is a good guy. He takes care of his own. I'm guessing I'm not the only one Griswold abused, and the sheriff probably realized Coach Denton knows that."

"You think he's telling the truth?" Ellie asked after Ryan had returned to his friends.

"Seems like it, although I don't think I'll take him off my list yet."

"You have a list?"

"More of a mental list, but I think it's time to take the one I started with Zak, add the stuff in my head, and modify the whole mess to see if anything pops. I was hoping Salinger would move on from Levi entirely and we could put this whole thing behind us."

"Yeah." Ellie sighed. "Me, too."

"Let's go find Zak and Charlie," I suggested. "Maybe he'll want to join us for a brainstorming session. We'll text Levi and ask him to meet us when he's finished with Salinger."

"If he doesn't end up back in jail," Ellie grumbled.

"Yeah, there's always that."

Chapter 14

Unfortunately, Salinger decided he had enough evidence to detain Levi. I was unwisely heading down to the sheriff's office to give the lug head a piece of my mind when I ran into Commissioner Cromwell, who kindly reminded me that if I didn't keep my nose out of things and let the sheriff investigate without my interference, I'd be out of a job. This, he reminded me, was my third and final warning.

Perhaps I should back up here. The last time Salinger and I locked horns, I sort of destroyed three months' of investigation and surveillance on the sheriff's part. We don't have a huge drug problem in Ashton Falls, but like any town in America, we do have drugs. About six months ago the incidence of overdose from a specific strain of street-level crack was on the rise. Salinger and his team spent months trying to trace the drugs back to their source.

On the very day they planned the bust, I responded to an animal cruelty call and, rather than reporting it to Salinger, as I was mandated to do, I broke into the house to free the dog, which was chained to a wall. In the process I discovered plans for a meeting between the local dealers and their source. When the dealers realized that I'd learned what I had, the buy was canceled. Salinger's surveillance efforts had been wasted.

I really did feel bad that I'd messed up Salinger's sting operation especially since it was the second time my bumbling attempt to do what I felt was the right thing resulted in a headache for him. The first time involved a car theft and the vehicle I actually helped steal (unwittingly of course) but that is a story for another day.

I took heed of the county commissioner's warning as I arranged to meet Zak and Ellie. I love my job more than I can convey. I believe that I serve a purpose in our community, and I know that many of the animals I've saved would be dead today if not for my dedication and hard work. I tell you this so you can understand the seriousness with which I took Cromwell's threat.

We decided to pick up sandwiches and have our meeting in the park. That way we could enjoy the Haunted Hamlet festivities while we talked. I decided to drop Charlie and Lambda off at the boathouse, while Ellie went ahead to the park to find a table and Zak picked up the food. By the time everyone arrived, the activities around us were in full swing.

"It's so strange to be sitting here in the middle of hundreds of kids dressed in costume and having the time of their lives, all the while the adults are talking about a gruesome murder," Ellie commented.

"Yeah, when I first woke up it didn't even register that today is Halloween," I supplied. "Happy Halloween, everyone." I lifted my soda in a toast.

"This has been the most surreal week of my life, and not in a good way," Ellie sighed. "Were you able to get in to see him?"

"No. I ran into Commissioner Cromwell on my way in to see Salinger, though."

"And?" Ellie knew about the commissioner's previous warnings.

"He kindly reminded me that if I stuck my nose into this even a tiny little bit, he'd have me fired, as previously promised."

"Can he do that?" Ellie wondered.

I shrugged. "I work for the county, he runs the county. I suppose if he wanted to fire me, he'd find a way. Salinger has him convinced that I'm a menace to the town and shouldn't be allowed to work in a position of authority."

"Maybe you should just stay out of this," Ellie said. "I'd hate for you to get fired."

I looked Ellie in the eye. "It's Levi. What would you do?"

"Yeah, I get it," she admitted. "But be careful. Let Zak and me do the legwork."

"Might be a good idea," I acknowledged. "Have you heard from the attorncy?" I asked Zak.

"He said that although it's weak, Salinger has put together a case. We know Levi has demonstrated many times in the past that he's protective of his kids. We know it's has recently come to his attention that Griswold was abusing at least some of his players. We know they had an altercation on the day Griswold was murdered. What we didn't know was that Levi has been arrested once before for assault."

I groaned. I knew about the assault charge. And it had been my fault. Once again I'd stuck my nose in where it didn't belong and gotten myself into a dangerous situation. Levi had come to my rescue, but in the process he'd been arrested. Ellie had been away at the time, and we'd decided not to tell her. In retrospect, that might not have been the best idea.

"Assault?" Ellie asked.

"It was a long time ago and probably wouldn't carry much weight with a jury, but for now it's enough to hold him," Zak said.

"Poor Levi," Ellie sympathized. "I feel so bad for him. I keep hoping Salinger will find a better suspect and move on."

"Which is why we're gathered together," I reminded everyone, "to generate a list of potential suspects we can check out. I brought paper." I held up a small notepad.

"Where do we even start?" Ellie sighed.

"If we continue with the assumption that the blackmail is related to the murder, I think we have to go back to looking at people who have access to Ashton Falls Events Committee letterhead," I pointed out.

"We aren't narrowing things down enough," Ellie stated the obvious. "Anyone could have gotten hold of that letterhead. There's a pile of it on the desk in Mom's office. Anyone could wander in and help himself to a piece."

I had to agree with Ellie. We needed something more, something that would cast a hook into our fish pond rather than a net. I felt like we were missing something obvious. Some small detail that, once revealed, would pull everything together.

"Coach Griswold is tall," I pointed out. "He was hit on the head hard enough to kill him. Whoever hit him had to be tall as well. I mean, I certainly couldn't hit the man in the head. The bat or whatever weapon I used would hit his shoulder at best."

"Lots of tall people in town," Zak argued, "including Levi."

"Yeah, I guess." I watched the kids lining up for the costume parade as I paused to let everything process. I couldn't help but let their enthusiasm transport me back to my own childhood, and the memories I had of what had to be my favorite holiday. I remembered dressing up in my fantasy of the moment, decorating a special trick-or-treat bag to hold the orgy of candy I planned to get, meeting up with my friends just as the sky was turning dark, then running from house to house as my über-protective dad watched from the sidelines.

I thought of the smell of wood smoke as friends and neighbors built fires to ward off the chill in the air. I remembered the feel of maple leaves, which had turned bright orange and red and fallen from the trees, crunching beneath my feet.

Every year I'd enter the costume parade, but I never won. Girls with mothers who crafted homemade costumes wooed the judges and took the prize. I remembered longing for something special that would set me apart but settling for ordinary because a store-bought costume was all my poor dad could manage. The more I longed to stand out, the more I seemed to blend in. Of course, my diminutive size didn't help. No wonder I seemed to forever get lost in the crowd.

"Is there anyone on that list who is tall now but started his football career as the team runt?" I asked.

"Michael Valdez went through an amazing growth spurt his freshman year, and so did Craig Masterson and Darien Wellington," Zak answered. "Why?"

"When we talked to Ryan today he mentioned that Griswold targeted the smallest kid on the team. It makes sense that if our killer is a student, and not a parent or mentor, he would have been a runt when he played for Griswold."

"When they played for Griswold the three boys I mentioned were the shortest kids on the team. All three are well over six feet today," Zak confirmed.

"And all three still live in town," Ellie added.

"It looks like we have a place to start," I concluded. "I'd be willing to bet that all three are here in town for the Haunted Hamlet. Should we split up?"

"Craig Masterson and Darien Wellington both signed up to work the haunted barn," Ellie informed us. "I'll head over and talk to them, if you want to try to find Michael. I don't remember seeing his name on any of the volunteer lists, but I'm sure his dad knows where he is."

"Okay, and we'll meet back here later," I said.

"Let Zak do the interviewing. You need to stay out of the spotlight," Ellie reminded me.

"Yes, Mom," I teased.

"Cromwell will fire you if he's given a good enough reason," Ellie reminded me.

"I know. I'll hang back and let you and Zak do the detective thing. If you think of anyone else, text me."

"Is your phone on?" Ellie asked.

"Yes, my phone is on. Geez. You forget a time or two and you're labeled for life."

Michael's dad, Frank, didn't know where he was, but he did confirm that he had been planning to hang out at the Haunted Hamlet with friends. He suggested we try the spooky maze, which was set up using hay bales in the field next to the haunted barn. The line was long, but not as long as I thought it might be.

Someone had decorated the entrance with creepy scarecrows and jack-o'-lanterns. I'd visited the maze before and knew that there was a hanging corpse, headless body, or evil skeleton around every turn. The maze was a fund-raiser for Gilda Reynolds's theater arts program. Kids from the program were dressed as various incarnations of zombies, vampires, witches, and other undead or evil beings. When you least expected it, one would jump out at you and send your heart rate racing.

One of the zombies at the entrance told us that Michael was helping out inside the maze, dressed as the grim reaper. Zak and I decided to head inside to see if we could find him. As we entered the main part of the maze, Zak took my hand. I told myself it was so that we wouldn't be separated, but I had to admit that I rather enjoyed the tingling sensation that worked its way up my arm and caused my heart to beat even faster. Not that I was falling for Zak. I mean up until a week ago I could barely stand the guy. I'd been under a lot of stress lately, which I assured myself was the *real* cause of my shortness of breath and sweaty palms.

"This is really fun," Zak said as he peeked around the intersection we'd come to. "I haven't done the haunted maze since I was in high school, and even then I just brought girls here to make out."

"Really? This place seems a little crowded to be a good make-out spot."

"Not if you come at night and carelessly take a wrong turn and get lost." Zak grinned.

I rolled my eyes. Guys were all the same. They had one thought and one thought only. Any deviation from that was usually a variation of the original thought. Still, I was having more fun than I'd had in a very long time. If Ellie and Levi got together, I'd need someone to keep me from feeling like a third wheel. Maybe Zak would make an acceptable fourth after all.

"There he is." I pointed toward a tall figure carrying a scythe.

We carefully made our way through the crowd to the corner of the maze, where Michael was waiting to jump out and scare people.

"Hi, Michael. Your dad told us you might be here. Can we talk to you for a minute?" I asked as we approached.

Michael looked around. "Yeah, okay. Let's head out. There's a shortcut through here."

Zak reminded me that I was supposed to hang back while he did the talking as we followed Michael through the maze toward an exit at the back. I agreed to watch from a distance. Normally waiting on the sidelines isn't my thing, but I love my job and am willing to put up with a certain amount of irritation in order to keep it.

"What's up?" Michael asked Zak.

"I guess you heard about Coach Griswold," Zak began.

"So?"

"We heard you used to play kiddie league for him."

"A long time ago," Michael confirmed.

"We spoke to another former kiddie league player who said Griswold had a tendency to pick on the smaller kids."

"Guy was an ass," Michael confirmed. "He not only picked on the smaller kids but he did everything he could to get them to quit. I hate to say it, but the world is better off without him."

"Do you know of anyone who might have hated the guy enough to kill him?" Zak asked.

"I know a *lot* of people who hated him enough to kill him," Michael confirmed. "If what you're really asking is if I know who killed him, though, the answer is no. Now if we're done, I really should get back."

"Yeah, okay. Thanks for your time."

"He knows something he's not saying," I suggested after Michael returned to the maze and I'd rejoined Zak.

"I got that feeling, too."

"Ellie texted. She has one more lead and wants to meet up in an hour," I informed him.

Zak looked at his watch. "You want to pick some pumpkins? The pumpkin patch is right around the corner, and we have time."

"You want to pick pumpkins?"

"We have an hour to kill. It's Halloween. Let's take a minute and do something fun."

"But Levi…"

"Unless you have another lead, there's nothing we can do until we meet Ellie," Zak reminded me.

"Okay." I smiled. I hate to confess it, but, although I always bought my pumpkins from the patch when I was growing up, I'd been so busy the past few years that I'd been getting my gourds at the market. It would be fun to wander the hillside where the patch was located, drink cider or hot spiced wine from the stand near the entrance, and search row after row, looking for the perfect candidate.

It was a quintessential fall day. The pumpkin patch was crowded but not packed, the sky was blue with just a few wispy clouds for atmosphere, and the red, orange, and yellow trees on the nearby hillside were breathtaking. The patch was part of a farm that featured a large pond, horses, cows, pigs, and chickens. It was fun to watch the kids chasing the chickens and feeding the larger animals.

"Remember our class trip in the seventh grade?" Zak asked after we'd paid our entrance fee and secured one of the wagons provided to transport your pumpkins from the patch to your car. "Levi caught a bunch of garter snakes and set them free in the pumpkin patch. There were girls running and screaming everywhere."

I laughed. "He never did get caught. Everyone figured the snake invasion was some natural occurrence brought on by recent rain."

"I had to admire the guy's ingenuity," Zak added. "He volunteered to help round up the harmless creatures, and all the girls thought he was a superhero or something. I couldn't believe how much play he got out of it."

"Levi always has had a way with the ladies," I agreed. "He has a theory that those of us of the fairer sex become much more agreeable when we're scared. It seems like he took every date he had in junior high to a horror movie or a roller coaster."

"What about this one?" Zak bent down to uncover a long, narrow pumpkin that would make an interesting jack-o'-lantern.

"Has potential," I agreed. "I think I'll get two: a big one, and one with an interesting or unusual shape. How about you?"

"I guess I'll get two as well." Zak picked the long, narrow pumpkin and set it in the wagon.

"They have a pick-your-own-apples orchard down near the road, if you want to pick a few up when we're done here," Zak said. "I've been thinking about making an apple pie."

"You bake?" I was surprised.

"I think you'll find I'm a man of many talents." He winked.

"I'll bet." I grinned.

Chapter 15

"I think we have a new suspect to add to our list," Ellie informed us the minute we met. "Gage Wexler.""

"I thought Gage left town to go to college," I said.

"He's back, apparently. I saw him hanging out with Craig, Darien, and some other kids. I tried to talk to them, but they took off."

I knew Gage had been troubled when he lived in Ashton Falls. He was in and out of juvenile hall throughout high school. I thought it odd that he was hanging out with kids so much younger than he was. Sure, they were all football players, but Craig and Darian were still in high school.

"Why would Gage kill Griswold?" Zak asked.

"I haven't worked it all out, but we know Gage was in a lot of trouble as a teen, we know he played kiddie league for Griswold, and we know he's back in town and hanging out with other kids we suspect of being former victims of Griswold," Ellie pointed out. "You mentioned the tagging in the house where you found the body. Gage was known for his illegal artwork. It just seems to fit."

"Yeah, it really does," I agreed.

"I'm pretty sure I heard them say they were heading to the haunted barn. I figured I'd meet you guys for backup and then head over. You up for a little interrogation?" Ellie looked at Zak.

"Absolutely."

"Zoe should stay here, though," Ellie said. "Maybe you can drop in on Warren before he leaves the hospital. That will give you a good alibi."

"Warren is leaving?" I asked.

"His family got an anonymous donation for the money they needed for Warren's surgery. They're moving him to a hospital down the hill tonight and hope to do the surgery tomorrow or Monday at the latest."

I glanced at Zak, who looked away, but I knew he had to have been the anonymous donor. Who else would have the kind of money it took to simply write a check to pay for surgery and a hospital stay? I guess technically my mother and her family would have the funds required to accomplish such a feat, but I also knew she'd left the area and had most likely never even heard of Warren Trent.

I hated to stay behind, but I did want to visit with Warren before he left, and I *really* wanted to keep my job.

"Okay," I agreed. "I'll head over to the hospital. Text me when you're done and we'll meet back up."

When I arrived at the hospital there were five boys sitting outside under a tree: Gage Wexler, Craig Masterson, Darian Wellington, Michael Valdez, who must have finished his gig at the haunted maze, and Cody Blunt, the mascot I'd met at Bryton Lake. All the boys were football players or involved in football and, I was willing to bet, all victims of Griswold's extreme coaching. I thought about calling Ellie to tell her that the boys she hoped to interview weren't at the haunted barn after all, but it occurred to me that the group could scatter before she and Zak had a chance to make their way here and the opportunity to talk to them would be lost. I thought about my job and how much it means to me, but as much as I love my job, I love Levi more. I walked toward the group.

"Hey, guys," I greeted.

"Hey, Zoe," Craig returned. "Did you come to see Warren? He told us you've been bringing him food."

"I'm afraid I didn't bring anything this time. I really came to talk to him about Coach Griswold's murder. They've arrested Coach Denton again. I guess they found fingerprints on the body," I lied, and carefully looked at each face as I did so. "It looks bad."

"Coach Denton didn't kill him," Darian spoke up.

I noticed that Gage, who stood next to him, nudged him with his elbow.

"Do you know who did?" I prompted.

Darian looked at the other boys. Cody was staring intently at the ground; Craig, and Michael were staring at one another, and Gage looked like he was preparing to run.

"We can't let Coach Denton go to jail for this," Darian insisted. He looked me in the eye. "We did it. All of us."

"Do you want to tell me what happened?"

I kept my eye on Gage as the other boys worked up the courage to speak.

"We didn't mean to kill him," Michael admitted.

"We were just trying to help Warren," Cody said in a quiet voice. "He's a good guy; he didn't deserve this."

"Go on," I prompted.

"When we found out Warren might not get the surgery he needed because of his family's financial situation, it occurred to us that Griswold really ought to be the one paying for it," Michael explained.

"I mean, he was the reason Warren was in the hospital in the first place. We couldn't prove it, but we knew it was true, so we came up with the blackmail plan," Darian added.

"I swear, all we were going to do was get enough money out of the guy to pay the hospital." Cody was crying. "We never meant for anyone to die."

"Okay, what happened?" I encouraged.

"Darian came up with the idea to blackmail the coach," Michael informed us. "Gage tagged his truck to emphasize the fact that we knew what had happened and weren't going to keep quiet. We used letterhead my dad had in his office, figuring Griswold would think one of the adults was blackmailing him. We thought he never would have gone along with the blackmail demand if he knew it was coming from a bunch of kids."

"And did he?" I asked. "Go along with it?"

"We thought he did." Darian paled.

"We told him to meet us at the Henderson place with ten thousand dollars. We knew he had that much because he used to brag all the time about the money he inherited," Craig informed us.

"But when he showed up he had a gun," Michael continued. "He was drunk and threatened to kill us if we didn't hand over whatever proof we had. The problem was, we didn't actually have any proof. He didn't believe us and pointed the gun right at Cody's head."

"I picked up a baseball bat we had been using to break stuff earlier in the night and hit him," Craig admitted. "I didn't mean to kill him, I swear. I just wanted to stop him from shooting Cody."

"It sounds like what was done was in self-defense," I reasoned. "You're a minor, and you were trying to help your friend. I'm sure Salinger will take that into consideration, but we have to tell him."

"I'm not a minor," Gage pointed out. "And I have a rap sheet."

"That could be a problem," I admitted.

"Besides, I wasn't anywhere near the Henderson house when this whole thing went down."

"Do you have proof of that?" I asked.

Gage hesitated.

"Maybe we can leave him out of it," Cody suggested. "All he did was tag the truck. Darian came up with the blackmail plan, Michael wrote the letter, and Craig is the one who actually hit him with the bat. The guys and I can vouch for the fact that he wasn't there when the whole thing went down."

"Let's go see Salinger. We can leave Gage out of it for now." I took a deep breath, mentally kissed my future good-bye, and made a decision. "I'll go with you."

Michael looked like he might faint, and the others looked as if they wanted to run, but they all followed me back into town.

Chapter 16

I sat on the beach, Charlie and Maggie at my side, and watched the moon rise over the lake. Somehow I'd survived the hardest couple of days of my life. I was physically and mentally depleted and unsure of how I'd be able to go on. After I'd accompanied the boys to the sheriff's office and they'd told their story to Salinger, I'd met Zak, Ellie, and a newly released Levi for a victory celebration. For that brief moment in time I really believed everything was going to be okay. That all the lives involved in this horrible affair would once again reach the equilibrium we'd all enjoyed prior to Griswold's murder.

Boy, was I wrong.

"Hey, there." Zak sat down next to me.

"Where'd you come from?" I asked.

"Down the beach. Your grandfather let Lambda and me move into the lake house while the paperwork is being completed. It looks like we're neighbors."

I smiled, finding I was glad for Zak's company. I laid my head against his shoulder and stared at the moonlight on the lake. I felt empty inside. Like a hollow shell of what once was and would never be again.

"How are you holding up?" Zak asked.

"I'm not," I answered honestly.

"Have you talked to Jeremy?" Zak asked.

"No. I can't. Not yet."

"You did the right thing."

"I know." In spite of the fact that I had managed to solve the case of Griswold's death in a calm and peaceful manner, Commissioner Cromwell had followed through on his threat to fire me. To make matters worse, he'd decided to close the Ashton Falls facility and provide satellite service from Bryton Lake. Not only was I out of a job but Jeremy was as well.

"Did they come for the animals?" I asked. Most of the animals had been adopted on Sunday, but there were several that weren't yet ready for homes. I prayed they'd be placed with loving families. I couldn't help but think of the mama cat and her babies. I'd grown fond of them during the short time that they'd been with us. At least I still had Maggie with me. She was doing better, gaining weight. I hated to think what would have happened to her if I hadn't brought her home.

"They did, but when they got there they found all the animals had been adopted."

I sat up and looked at Zak. "Adopted? All of them? By whom?"

"Me, actually," he confessed. "For the short-term, anyway. Even I don't have room for seven dogs, three cats, and four kittens."

"You have them at your house?"

"For now. I need to find them homes." Zak used his thumb to wipe away the tear trailing down my face. "I was sort of hoping you would help."

"And the wild animals?" I hated to even ask.

"Released or relocated. I have a raccoon in one of my extra bedrooms."

I smiled.

"I'm not sure I should bring this up, but I actually came down the beach because I have news," Zak informed me.

"What kind of news?"

"It's about Griswold's murder. Craig Masterson didn't kill the guy. Once the autopsy was completed they found that, although Craig did hit Griswold, the blow he delivered didn't kill him. Someone came along after the boys left and finished the job."

"I know."

"You do?"

"I've had a few days to think about things, and there was something that just wasn't adding up."

"Such as?"

"First of all, I found Griswold's body in the basement. The boys didn't mention anything about dragging him down there. They told Salinger they lured him to the house on the pretext of having proof that he'd run Warren off the road. Their goal was to get the money to pay for Warren's medical bills, but when Griswold turned on them Craig hit him over the head with a bat. They freaked when they saw the blood and ran."

"So the question is, how did Griswold get to the basement?"

"Exactly. I also realized that Griswold's body had suffered multiple fractures which most likely occurred when he was drug down the stairs. And what about the dog that brought me to the house in the first place? Where did he come from, and how did he get locked in the basement?"

"So you think whoever finished the job dragged the body to the basement and the dog was trapped inside in the process."

"Exactly."

"Okay, who?"

"I realized that whoever came along and finished the job would have had to have known the boys were meeting Griswold in the Henderson house. Initially, the only person I could think of who knew the guys were meeting him was—"

"Gage," Zak finished for me.

"He said he wasn't with the guys when the whole thing went down and they backed him up, but he never really said where he was at the time."

"Perhaps we should ask him."

"I did."

Zak looked surprised.

"What? Do you think I've been doing nothing other than sitting around moping for the past few days?"

"Actually, that's exactly what I thought."

"Okay, I will admit that moping has been the main course on the Zoe menu, but I managed to do a little investigating as well. I was able to catch Gage just as he was preparing to leave to go back to college. I confronted him about the murder, which he adamantly denied having any involvement in."

"He could be lying," Zak pointed out.

"He could have been, but he has a pretty solid alibi."

"Such as?" Zak wondered.

"He was in the process of relieving Donovan's of some of our pesky inventory. My dad had security cameras installed a couple of years ago, after that rash of robberies we had. When Gage confessed that his alibi to murder was petty theft I had my dad look at the tapes."

"So Gage is the random bandit?"

"It would seem. The security tape my dad has is time and date stamped, so we're pretty sure based on the time line the other boys provided that Gage couldn't have been involved in Griswold's murder."

"But you said someone went back after the boys left and killed Griswold. Maybe Gage ended a night of breaking and entering with murder," Zak suggested.

"I considered that, but then I realized that the one piece of the puzzle that didn't really fit was the dog. Someone had to have come in the front door and left it open, allowing the dog to get in while the killer dragged the body to the basement. The dog must have wandered into the basement when the killer went into the bathroom to wash up."

"How do you know the killer washed up?"

"I remembered seeing blood in the sink."

"Okay, I'm with you so far. The dog wanders into the basement while the killer is in the bathroom."

"Exactly. The killer leaves the bathroom and then remembers the basement door. The killer returns to the basement and closes the door, trapping the dog inside. The killer then leaves without realizing the dog has been trapped."

"The dog starts howling and disturbs the neighbors," Zak supplied. "You go to investigate and find the body."

"Bingo."

"Okay, that makes sense, but how does that help us identify the killer?"

"I checked around, and none of the neighbors claimed to know who the dog belonged to. I asked myself, if he hadn't come from the neighborhood around the Henderson place, where *had* he come from?"

"You think the killer brought him? Whoever murdered Griswold probably left the dog in the car, went in, and finished what the boys started, and then accidentally locked the dog in the basement. Wouldn't the killer notice the dog was missing?" Zak asked.

"Probably, if she knew she had the dog."

"Come again?"

"What if the person who killed Griswold drives a truck, and the dog jumped into the back without the killer noticing? Charlie used to do that to me before I had the camper shell. When he was a pup there were times he'd notice I was going somewhere and hop in when I wasn't looking. Maybe the dog owner didn't miss the dog until later."

"So find out who owns the dog and you find the killer. How do we do that?" Zak asked.

"I already know. I decided I wasn't going to come forward with my theory unless evidence supported the idea that Craig hadn't killed Griswold. Salinger has already decided not to press charges against Craig for the murder, because he clearly hit him in self-defense. All the boys are looking at attempted blackmail charges, but given the circumstances, I think Salinger would have gone easy on them. In my mind the path of least resistance was to let sleeping dogs lie."

Zak looked at me. "The killer is someone you want to protect. It isn't Levi?"

"No. Not Levi. I know this individual should answer for Griswold's murder, but to be honest, if he'd done to me what he did to this person, I'd have killed him, too."

"Do I even want to know?" Zak wondered.

"Salinger will figure it out. It's only a matter of time, now that he realizes that Craig didn't kill the man. It'll be best if this person turns herself in."

"Okay," Zak said. "Who killed the bastard?"

"The person he hurt the most. For years Griswold abused the weaker kids on his team in order to get them to quit. Most of the kids grew up and got over it, but there's one unwanted player from whom he took something that can't be returned."

Zak looked shocked as the pieces fell into place. "Samantha Collins."

I nodded my head.

"He raped her?"

"He was outraged that she was allowed to join the team. His harassment of her began on day one and intensified as she became even more determined to stay on the team. To make matters worse, most of the guys didn't want her on the team either, so they supported Griswold in his harassment. Cody Blunt was one of the few members of the team who stuck up for her. After the guys left Cody called Samantha and told her they'd killed him."

"But she went to check for herself," Zak guessed. "Only Griswold wasn't dead, just unconscious. Oh, man. What are we going to do?"

"What we have to do. Samantha's parents weren't supportive when she complained of being bullied by Griswold, so she was afraid to talk to them when Griswold...well, you know. In fact until I spoke to her she'd never told anyone about the rape. I wanted her to talk to her parents, but she refused, so I set her up with counseling. I hoped that would be enough to get her through this, but with this new evidence I guess we'll need to talk her into turning herself in and hope that Salinger has a soul beneath his gruff exterior."

"I'll talk to her parents once everything is out in the open," Zak offered. "Make sure she has the best attorney money can buy."

"That's really nice of you, but let's hope it doesn't get that far. Samantha needs counseling, not jail time. Hopefully Salinger and the DA will see it that way."

"I can't see how they wouldn't."

I leaned my head against Zak's shoulder. This whole thing had really put things in perspective. Before I found out about the hell Samantha had gone through in the past few months, I felt like losing my job was the worst thing that had ever happened. Now it is, simply, *something* that happened. I don't know what the future holds for either of us, but my intuition tells me that everything is going to work out okay.

Zoe's Treasure Hunt

Chapter 1

We've all had them. Those days that start off in one place and end up somewhere else entirely. On the day in question, Charlie and I decided to stop off at the hospital to visit one of our favorite patients, eight-year-old Tommy Porter. Tommy had been through a difficult spell, spending a lot more time in the hospital than an eight-year-old should. As a trained therapy dog, Charlie was used to providing just the right kind of comfort to get a person through a rough patch, and my intuition told me that someone at the hospital—I assumed Tommy—was in desperate need of Charlie's special brand of care.

"Well, if it isn't Zoe Donovan and her wonder dog Charlie," I was greeted by Ryder Westlake, the doctor responsible for getting the hospital board to approve the therapy dog program in the first place. "I was just thinking that I might call you to ask you to come by, and here you are. It's almost like you can read minds."

"Oh, I can," I teased the handsome man with the dark hair and blue eyes. "Actually, Charlie wanted to stop by to check in on Tommy."

"I'm happy to say that Tommy is doing better. His mother picked him up and took him home this morning. But I do have a patient I'd like you to look in on. His name is Burton Ozwald. He goes by Oz. He had a mild heart attack, which I believe he will recover from, but he seems to be overly agitated. He keeps mentioning that he needs to get out of here before it's too late. I've tried to find out what's on his mind, as have the nurses, but he isn't saying anything else. Maybe he'll talk to you."

"I'll give it a try. What room is he in?"

"Two-o-four."

Charlie and I poked our heads in and said hi to a few of the other patients as we made our way to the second floor. The Ashton Falls Community Hospital isn't large, so Charlie and I try to check in on all the patients who are permitted to have visitors whenever we come by. Most of them tell us that Charlie's adorable face brings sunshine to their otherwise dark day.

"Mr. Ozwald," I greeted as I stood near the entry, waiting for permission to proceed the rest of the way into the room.

"Just Oz. What can I do for you?"

"My dog Charlie and I are on the premises visiting those we can. I wondered if you'd like us to come in for a few minutes."

The frail man with thin white hair covering a slightly balding head seemed to be considering my offer. He looked at me and then at Charlie and shrugged. "Sure, I guess. I like dogs."

Charlie and I entered the room. I asked if it was okay for Charlie to get up onto the bed, and when we got permission I instructed him to do so, making certain that he didn't bother any of the tubes or plugs attached to the old man. Charlie had been specially trained to lie perfectly still while providing doggy warmth and comfort to those he visited.

"So you're a visitor to our town," I began.

"Yup."

"Family in the area?"

"Nope."

"So you're visiting friends?"

"Nope."

"I imagine you're looking forward to doing a bit of sightseeing while at the lake?"

"Nope."

"Passing through?"

"Nope."

I could see that starting a conversation with this man was going to be a challenge.

"November is a good month to visit, whatever your reason," I informed him. "The summer visitors have left and the skiers who show up in droves during the winter have yet to arrive. There are a lot of good discounts for lodging and dining. Although I guess that isn't a huge concern of yours at this particular time."

"Nope."

I looked at Charlie, who was lying at Oz's side. He looked back at me, and I swear, if dogs could roll their eyes, he'd be rolling his. Okay, so I wasn't off to a great start with the mysterious visitor to our area, but at least I was trying. Charlie was just lying there, doing nothing to help get the ball rolling.

"It seems like you might not feel up to talking right now. Maybe Charlie and I could come by later, when you're feeling better."

"Won't be here later."

"But I was told you'd suffered a heart attack, which I'm sure will require at least a short stay. Charlie and I can come by any time you'd like."

The man looked at me with pale blue eyes that might have been darker at one point but had faded with age. "I appreciate that, and it seems like your dog is a nice enough sort, but I really need to be on my way. I tried telling the doctor that I was fine and wanted to check myself out, but apparently he isn't listening to what I'm saying."

I was trying to figure out what to say to get the old man to open up to me when Charlie jumped off the bed. He trotted over to a chair in the corner, where Oz's personal belongings were stacked. A brown corduroy coat hung over the back of the chair. Charlie stuck his nose into the pocket and came trotting back with a yellowed envelope in his mouth.

"Charlie, what are you doing?" I scolded. "I'm sorry." I turned to the man in the hospital bed. "I don't know what's gotten into Charlie. He's never done anything like that before."

Charlie hopped up on the bed, put the envelope on the man's chest, and then lay down quietly beside him as he had before.

The man looked shocked by Charlie's actions. He picked up the envelope with one gnarled hand while he petted Charlie with the other. "Seems you got yourself a right smart little dog. I had a smart dog like Charlie once. Her name was Antonia. She passed a few years ago."

"I'm so sorry."

"She had a good life and we said our good-byes. It was her time and she seemed to know it. She brought me a lot of comfort during her life, but one of the most important things she did for me was to show me how to die."

I frowned. "What do you mean?"

"She didn't fight it. She almost welcomed it. She knew her time had arrived, so she said her good-byes and then retreated to her corner and let the end come. I remember thinking at the time that I wanted to go the same way. I wanted to welcome the next life rather than fighting for every last breath in this one. I know the doc says my heart attack was minor, but I know my time is near. A person knows these things. I'd say I have less than a month left, and I accept that. There's just one last thing I need to do."

"Which is why you came to Ashton Falls," I realized.

"I have a granddaughter," the man began. "She looks a lot like you. Smart little thing. Her parents died when she was young, so my Patty and I raised her until Patty died when Sarah was twelve. After that it was just the two of us. Patty and I had children late in life, so we were older than most grandparents, but we loved spending as much time as we could with our little angel."

"Loved? Did something happen to her?"

"No," the old man informed me, "nothing happened to her. She just grew up and went out into the world to make her own way. She's a senior in college and wants more than anything to go to medical school when she graduates. Like I mentioned before, she's a smart girl, and I know she can do anything she sets her mind to. Problem is, medical school is expensive, and I'm afraid I'm not in a position to help her out the way I'd like."

"There are scholarships," I suggested.

"Maybe. But Sarah is family, and one ought to do for family. I know I won't be here by the time she graduates in the spring, but I want to be sure she has everything she needs to take the next step in her life, so I've come to Devil's Den to claim my inheritance."

I suppose this is a good place to mention that the original name for the mining camp where Ashton

Falls now sits was Devil's Den. Not a cozy name, to be sure, but probably a bit more accurate than the somewhat pretentious Ashton Falls, a name given to the town by Ashton Montgomery, a multimillionaire and my great-grandfather on my mother's side.

"Your inheritance?" I asked.

"My grandfather was a miner back in the day when the area was known as Devil's Den. I never knew him, but from what my father told me, he was an irresponsible SOB who left his family and lived his life in the pursuit of gold. My dad never talked about him, and as far as I know he hadn't been in contact with him since he left to follow the gold rush. When my dad died twenty years ago I found this letter my grandfather sent to him at some point. It says he left my dad a bag of gold and provided instructions of sorts on how to find it. I never followed up on it. My dad made it sound like my grandfather was a flake, but when Sarah came to me with her idea of going to medical school I realized it was worth the trip out here to try to find the gold I figure is rightfully mine."

"You said your grandfather left it for your dad. When was that?"

"The letter was postmarked in April 1940."

"That's a long time ago. Do you think the gold is still where your grandfather left it?"

"I figure it has to be. Seems that's the only way my Sarah will be able to pursue her dream. The reality is that I have nothing to lose by looking for it." The man picked up the letter Charlie had brought him.

"Can I help?" I offered.

The man looked me up and down. "I suppose you seem the honest sort."

"I am," I assured him. "A lot has changed since your grandfather hid the gold, so it might not be all that easy to follow the instructions he left, but I'm willing to try. I've lived in Ashton Falls my whole life and I know the area better than most."

The man seemed to come to a decision. He handed me the letter, which ended with a riddle that gave clues to things that most likely no longer existed, but I'd told Oz I'd help him, and I intended to do just that. I read the riddle aloud:

"To begin the quest
I give to you
A maiden's breast
As the initial clue.

"'A maiden's breast'?" I asked. "Did your father have any idea what maiden his father was referring to?"

"He didn't, but I assume he was speaking of a landmark of some type, not an actual maiden."

"Okay, I'll see what I can do." I read the clue again. "It looks like your grandfather might have laid out an entire treasure hunt. It states that there's an initial clue that has to do with a maiden's breast. It sounds like we'll find another clue that will most likely lead to something else after we find the maiden's breast."

"That's the way I read it as well."

"My pappy has lived in the area for a long time. Is it okay if I share this with him?"

Oz seemed to consider my question. "I guess at this point I'm at your mercy. I know we just met, but my instinct tells me that I can trust you, so I guess I'll trust those you trust as well."

I smiled and placed my hand over his wrinkled one. "I'll see what I can find out and then I'll come back to see you in the morning. You have to promise me that you'll do everything the doctors and nurses tell you to do in the meantime."

"I will. I'll see you in the morning."

After Charlie and I left the hospital we headed to Donovan's, the general store my pappy built and my dad now runs. I knew Pappy and a couple of his friends liked to play chess in the seating area on cold winter mornings, and chances were that the big brown chair near the potbellied stove was where I'd find him.

It was beginning to snow. Not large fluffy flakes that would cover the ground, but small flurries that hinted at a larger storm to come. Charlie and I had dressed warm for the season, so I wasn't overly concerned that the drop in temperature that always accompanied a storm would interfere with the promise we'd made to Oz.

"Mornin', Pappy." I kissed him on the cheek before greeting his two friends, Nick Benson, a retired doctor, and Ethan Carlton, a retired history professor.

"What are you and Charlie up to on this fine morning?" Pappy asked.

"A treasure hunt, actually."

Pappy looked surprised. "A treasure hunt?"

I explained about Oz and his quest to find the gold his grandfather had left to his father, which he wanted to find to help his granddaughter pay for medical school.

"Seems like it's going to be tough to follow clues that are over seventy years old," Pappy commented.

"Perhaps. But I promised to try and I'm going to do just that. I don't suppose you'd want to help me? All of you?" I looked at the other men.

"I'm game," Ethan spoke up.

"Me too," Nick added. "It's not like I have a lot going on."

"Your dad had to go out to run a few errands, so I told him I'd watch the place, but I'm in once he gets back. Any idea what this maiden's breast refers to?"

"I have no idea," I said. "Oz didn't know either. I figure it has to be some sort of landmark. Maybe a hill shaped like a maiden's breast, or a painting hanging on a wall in the old bordello, or maybe a statue or something? I really have no idea how to narrow it down."

"You know," Ethan began, "when I'm researching a local legend, I usually begin with a Google search, and if that doesn't provide what I'm looking for, I look at letters and journals from the time period I'm researching. There are quite a few old documents in the library. I'm fairly certain that many of them date back to the old mining camp. If I remember correctly the camp was occupied from around 1880 until the gold dried up in the mid 1940s."

"Oz said the letter was dated in April of 1940," I informed the men.

"I have my laptop in my car," Nick offered, "and the library has Internet service. Maybe we should move this treasure hunt over there. We can see what Google turns up, and then maybe we can have Hazel help us sort through the documents the library has in its possession."

"The three of you go on ahead and I'll join you when Hank gets back," Pappy said.

Nick, Ethan, Charlie, and I headed over to the library. The flurries that had been floating about all morning had stopped, but the dark clouds over the summit hinted at the much bigger storm that was about to make its presence known. I love this time of year. There's an encompassing quiet that seems to prevail, as if a giant dome has surrounded us, and we leave behind the hustle and bustle of the long days of summer. As I looked toward the summit in anticipation of the first real storm of the season, I let the serenity around me seep into my consciousness. I braked gently as a squirrel scurried across the road, completely oblivious to the danger presented by my truck as he frantically collected nuts and seeds for the long winter ahead.

When we arrived at the library we filled Hazel Hampton, the town librarian, in on our quest. Luckily, it was a slow time of day and we were the only ones occupying the reference section of the small building.

"You said the riddle refers to a maiden's breast?" Hazel asked.

I unfolded the letter and read the clue aloud:

"To begin the quest
I give to you
A maiden's breast
As the initial clue."

"You know, your theory that it could refer to a painting or sculpture is a good one," Hazel commented. "There are photos in one of these books on the town before Ashton Montgomery bought and modernized it. Maybe we can find a photo that will point us in the right direction."

Hazel handed us each a stack of books that contained old photos that had yellowed with age. It was really interesting, trying to pick out the locations of the buildings in the photos based on the surrounding countryside. Ashton had torn down many of the old buildings and modernized others, creating a completely different landscape. It was hard to imagine that many of the photos had been taken in locations I frequented every day.

"Look at this photo of Main Street." I pushed a book across the table so the others could see what I was looking at. "You'd never even know it was the same place if it weren't for the lake to the south of the road and Pickler's Peak in the background. This building here," I pointed to a saloon, "looks like it sat in the same spot the library now occupies."

"It is the same location," Hazel confirmed. "I have a photo of the old saloon around here somewhere." She began sorting through the albums on the table. There was something comforting about sitting around an oblong table with good friends as we tried to unravel a mystery on a cold winter's day.

"Here it is." Hazel opened one of the books. "I did a bit of research for the town's fiftieth anniversary celebration. I wanted to know what existed in the space now occupied by the library before this building was erected. It seems there was a two-story structure in this spot, which included a saloon on the first floor and bedrooms upstairs, where the girls entertained the men who had come in from the mines."

I studied the photo. It looked like something out of the old west. The *very* old west. "How long ago was this photo taken?" I asked.

"I believe it was taken in the 1930s. Do we know when this man's grandfather hid the gold?"

"The letter was dated April 1940," I replied.

"The old mining camp closed down around 1945 and most of the residents had moved on by 1950. The town was totally deserted and had been for a while by the time Ashton bought it in 1955. He tore down a lot of the old buildings when he built Ashton Falls, and I know that several of the buildings were damaged before that, during the forest fire of 1952. Still, if the letter was written in 1940, it stands to reason that the town looked pretty much the way it does in these photos when the gold was hidden."

I picked up another of Hazel's books and continued to look for something—anything—that might point us in a direction. The odds of actually finding Oz's gold were remote, but so far looking for it sure had been fun.

"Look at this." I pointed to a photo that showed the masthead of a mermaid, like the ones you'd find on an old ship, attached to the end of the bar. "Would this masthead have been here when Oz's grandfather left the gold?"

Hazel frowned. "I remember reading about that somewhere." She got up and went over to the section of the library where old documents, including some old journals left by miners, were kept. She pulled a book off the shelf and carefully thumbed through it while the rest of us waited.

"Yes, here it is. The masthead was brought to Devil's Den by a man named Warren Goldberg in 1908. It seems he owned a sailing vessel at one time that he sold to fund his journey west. This article says that while he sold the boat to an exporter, he kept the masthead, which held special meaning for him." Hazel looked up from the book she was reading. "The masthead was actually a carving that was made to look like his fiancée, who died before the couple could be married. Warren reportedly carted the large wooden object all the way to Devil's Den, where he hoped to start a new life."

"So how did the masthead end up in the bar?" I asked.

"I don't really know," Hazel admitted. "This journal entry simply says that the ship the masthead was originally carved for had been christened the *Maiden Marilyn*. After the masthead was built into the bar the men simply referred to it as the Maiden."

I felt a moment of excitement that was quickly replaced by a much longer one of despair. "Do we know whatever happened to the Maiden?" If she did hold the clue, her place in the bar had been long past.

"Actually, we do know what happened to her," Ethan joined in. "I've been sitting here trying to figure out where I've seen this before. It was attached to the back wall in the Ashton Falls Museum, but it had begun to deteriorate, so it was moved into storage. I believe I can get us access to have a look."

"Look at what?" Pappy walked in while Ethan was speaking.

"The *Maiden*. Want to come?"

The four of us thanked Hazel for her help and set off with Charlie for the museum. The facility was only open on weekends during the off season, but Ethan arranged for us to meet the man who managed the exhibit. Although he agreed to let us have a look at the masthead, I held little hope that we'd actually find the next clue to the puzzle. After all, we had no way of knowing if the maiden in the riddle and the Maiden in the bar even referred to the same thing. And even if it did, it had been years since Oz's grandfather wrote the letter to his son, and the masthead had been moved several times. If there ever was a clue it would probably be long gone by now.

We thanked the museum administrator for taking time out of his day to meet with us, and he showed us to the dusty room that housed relics that weren't displayed for one reason or another. The masthead, which wasn't as large as I'd thought it would be, was in the corner of the room, covered with a waterproof tarp.

The administrator turned on the overhead light and removed the covering. "Not sure what you're looking to find. The thing isn't in very good shape."

Ethan walked toward the object and looked it over from a distance. "May I?" He indicated that he would like to touch the masthead, perhaps move it around a bit.

"Go ahead. It's not like it's the *Venus de Milo*. My programs on, so I'm going to get back to the house. Lock up when you leave."

"I will," Ethan promised.

I stood just behind Ethan as he examined the artifact. I wanted to tell him to get out of the way and let me have a look, but he did have a doctorate in history, and I had a doctorate in nothing.

"This really is a spectacular piece of art," Ethan commented.

"Really?" It just looked like a partially rotted piece of wood with peeling paint to me.

"The detail work on the sculpture is quite intricate. It seems obvious to me that the man who carved the figure went to a lot of effort to get it just right. It seems odd that it ended up in a bar."

Ethan continued to caress the figure as he examined it. "I know this is going to sound odd, but I get the feeling that the man who carved this loved the woman it represented very much. I don't see him bringing it all the way west and then displaying it in a bar for men to ogle and defile. Something doesn't add up."

"Maybe the man who owned the masthead is the same one who owned the bar," I speculated.

"I suppose there are ways to figure out who actually owned the bar," Pappy added.

"It still seems odd that the man would put a carving of his dead fiancée in the bar even if he owned it," Nick asserted.

"Maybe the guy who brought the masthead west sold it to buy supplies or lost it in a poker game," I suggested. "I doubt we'll ever know what really happened."

"Well, I'll be," Ethan said a few minutes later. He had cupped the breast of the masthead and a drawer at the bottom of the carving popped open.

"A secret drawer," I gasped.

"With a piece of paper in it," Ethan added. He removed the paper and handed it to me.

"I can't believe we actually found something," I exclaimed. "When we began this journey I figured that it was a long shot that there even was a treasure to find, but a real clue means there probably is, or at least was, a real bag of gold."

"Just like in the movies," Ethan commented.

"I always wanted to go on a treasure hunt when I was a kid." Nick leaned over my shoulder and tried to get a look at the paper I held.

"It is pretty exciting," Pappy agreed. "What does the paper from the drawer say?"

I read it out loud:

"To find what's next
You must reveal
The hidden text
In the medic's seal.

"The medic's seal?" I asked.

"They're usually round with words and perhaps a symbol that states the motto of a particular organization or individual," Ethan explained. "I'm going to assume in this case that the clue refers to a symbol of sorts that might have been hanging on the wall at the local clinic."

The hospital in Ashton Falls hadn't been around that long ago, and the only older medical facility in town was a one-room clinic with a single doctor.

"So how do we get a look at this seal?" I asked.

"Maybe Hazel can find a photo of it in one of her books," Pappy said.

"Okay, I guess we go back to the library," I decided.

I was having more fun than I had in a long time, but I had to wonder why Oz's grandfather had gone to all the trouble of putting together this treasure hunt. Based on what I had read in the letter, the man was sick and knew he was going to die. If he had gold to send to his son, why not just put it in a bank or other secure repository and send his son a letter telling him how to find it? Oz had indicated that his father and grandfather had had a falling out, so I thought the gold might have been meant for the grandson all along. Still, leaving it in some kind of trust would have been a whole lot easier.

By the time we got back to the library Hazel was getting ready to close for the day, but she agreed to stay with us while we attempted to find a photo of the seal referred to in the riddle. It was a good thing Hazel was familiar with the old documents left in her care; she quickly narrowed down which documents we should examine for our answers.

I had the oddest feeling as I looked through the photos, letters, and documents of the men who had first settled this area. It was like I was really seeing my home for the first time. Ashton Falls is a cute town nestled in the nook of the nearby mountains, where the terrain flattens out a bit at the lake. The town is a cozy mountain hamlet Ashton Montgomery fashioned to serve as a mecca for tourism and recreation.

They teach us in school that the land where the town sits was once occupied by a mining camp known as Devil's Den. I'm not sure what I thought it was like, but as I looked at the photos of the teeny, tiny one-room homes, dirt streets, and plentiful saloons, I realized that the town I'd imagined wasn't an accurate representation of the reality of Devil's Den at all.

"Look at this house." I held up one of the books. "The entire thing can't be more than four hundred square feet. There's no electricity or running water, and the only heat is from a wood stove. How did people live like that?"

"Folks made do with what they had," Pappy said. "Most of the men who came to the area were single, though I suppose a few had wives and children because I noticed a photo of a one-room schoolhouse a while back."

"What's so odd to me is that Devil's Den existed in fairly modern times. Things like electricity existed then, so why did the majority of these people do without?" I asked.

"There weren't any roads or utilities here until Ashton bought the land and modernized the area," Pappy pointed out. "I realize that seems odd, but the community of Devil's Den was way up on the mountain, and until Ashton footed the expense to run electrical wires up the mountain, the community was cut off from the services available in Bryton Lake. And there are still homes in the county that use generators for power and access wells for their water supply."

"Yeah, I guess you're right. These photos have really brought home how recently the area was settled in comparison to the rest of the state."

"Oh, look; here's a photo of the old schoolhouse," Hazel announced. "It says here that the teacher's name was Wilma Brandywine. She doesn't look a day over eighteen."

I took the album Hazel handed me, which was opened to a black-and-white photo that showed the one-room schoolhouse, which seemed to be painted white with black trim, with a centrally located bell tower and a charming covered front porch. Standing in front of the building was a young woman with long dark hair wearing a dress that nearly covered the sturdy boots she was wearing. She was standing with a group of children ranging in age, I would guess, from five to fifteen. The children looked happy, most of them smiling at whoever had taken the photo.

As I turned the pages of the album I felt a special affinity for the men, women, and children who were shown living their lives, going to jobs, attending church and school, and eventually dying. One photo of a baby in the arms of a young mother especially touched my heart. It must have been so difficult to keep young children safe and healthy when there were so many challenges presented in day-to-day life.

"You know, the old cemetery is still there," I said as I continued to look at the photos. "It's pretty overgrown, but Charlie and I hike up there sometimes and look at the old gravestones. There are some that date back to the mid-1800s. I wonder if Warren Goldberg or Wilma Brandywine are buried there."

"It might be interesting to take a look, now that we have names and faces," Hazel added. "I've thought a few times about cleaning up the brush and maybe planting a few flowers to brighten the place up a bit. I'm not sure how many folks still visit that old cemetery. Probably not a lot. You can only access the area on foot, and everyone buried there has been gone for quite some time."

Oz said his grandfather had sent the letter shortly before he died. I couldn't help but wonder if I'd find a gravestone with the last name of Ozwald if I went up and looked. Had he been loved and buried with care or forgotten in an unmarked grave?

"I found a photo of the exterior of the clinic," Ethan announced. "Unfortunately, there isn't a photo of the seal referred to in the second clue."

"I guess all we can do is keep looking. You don't think the hospital would have something like that on display?" I asked.

"You know, they might," Nick said.

"I planned to go by to check on Oz in the morning. I can talk with Dr. Westlake. Should we continue this quest in the morning?"

"I'm in," everyone agreed.

Chapter 2

The next morning Charlie and I headed to the hospital first thing after breakfast. I hoped to have this mystery wrapped up by the end of the day. As much as I was enjoying the journey, I did have my own life to get back to, and I knew Oz would feel better once he'd accomplished his mission.

Luckily, Dr. Westlake was on duty when I arrived. There are other doctors who serve the hospital, but Ryder is by far the friendliest and most cooperative. He had supported my crazy ideas in the past and I hoped he would support my idea to help Oz find his gold.

"Morning, Zoe. You're here two days in a row. You and Charlie must have really hit it off with our new patient. Any luck figuring out why he's so anxious to get out of here?"

I explained briefly about the gold and our treasure hunt to help Oz find it. I asked Ryder to keep it to himself; I wasn't sure how Oz would feel about the good doctor knowing what was going on, but I needed his help to find the seal.

"Actually, we do have some stuff from the old clinic," Dr. Westlake said. "Old files and documents, that sort of thing. They're stored in a corner of the file room. If you promise not to rat me out to the nurse on duty, who happens to be a stickler for the rules, I guess I could let you in to have a look."

"Thanks; that would be great, and Charlie and I plan to pay a visit to Oz afterward."

I followed Dr. Westlake through the hospital, up the back stairs, and to the end of the hall on the second floor. He unlocked a door, flicked on a light, and showed me inside. The room was filled with rows and rows of fireproof file cabinets. I imagined that most contained patient records. In the back corner of the room were boxes stacked almost to the ceiling. Ryder escorted me to the pile and informed me that the stuff from the old clinic was inside those boxes.

"Wow, that's a lot of boxes," I said.

"Yeah, and they aren't all that organized. I'm afraid looking for a specific document could take days. I'd stay to help you, but I have rounds to get to."

I considered what to do. "The seal I'm looking for was most likely displayed on a wall, so I imagine it was framed. Would items such as that be kept elsewhere?"

Dr. Westlake thought about it. "I'm not sure. I haven't noticed any old furnishings from the clinic, although," he smiled, "there are a few photos of the old clinic displayed in the waiting room outside of emergency. If I were you, I'd start there and then come back to the boxes if you need to."

"Thanks. I'll do that."

I followed Dr. Westlake back out of the room. He continued down the hall and I headed toward the waiting room he'd mentioned. As promised, there were photos of the hospital during various phases of its existence, including several from the clinic in Devil's Den. My heart leapt with hope as I spotted a photo of the interior of the one-room clinic. There was one framed photo that was too small to make out. What I needed was a magnifying glass.

I looked around to make sure Nurse By the Rules wasn't watching and then took the photo off the wall. Then I headed back downstairs to see if the good doctor could help me read that which was otherwise too small to make out.

"Do you happen to have a microscope?" I asked when I'd caught up with Ryder.

"Of course I have a microscope. This is a hospital," he pointed out. "What do you need?"

I showed him the photo. "I think that may be the seal on the wall, but I can't make it out. I hoped if we were able to enlarge it, we could see what it says."

Ryder took the photo. He also looked around to make sure the nurse on duty wasn't lurking. You'd think it was the doctors who were in charge in a hospital, but everyone knows that it's actually the nurses who can make life pleasant or otherwise. After he confirmed we were alone, he led me down the hall to the lab. He took the photo out of the frame and looked at it through his instrument.

"It says *legatum sit amet*."

"Huh?"

"It's Latin. It means 'life is love's legacy.'"

"'Life is love's legacy'? What does that mean?"

"I really don't know. It's a nice sentiment, though. At the bottom of the seal it says LIV, all in caps."

"Dr. Westlake, please report to the second-floor nurses' station," a female voice said over the intercom system.

"I have to go," Dr. Westlake informed me. "If you could put this back before you leave that would be great." He handed me the photo.

I put the photo back into the frame and then headed back down the hall to replace it in the waiting room. Life is love's legacy? What in the heck did that mean, and how would it help me to find the next clue, if there was another clue to find?

I headed back toward Oz's room. Maybe he knew something that could shed some light on the mystery of the cryptic clue.

"I'm afraid Mr. Ozwald can't have visitors right now," the nurse at the desk informed me as I headed toward the closed door

"I thought it was visiting hours."

"It is, but I'm afraid Mr. Ozwald has suffered a setback. The doctor is in with him right now. I suggest you check back this afternoon."

I frowned "Setback?"

"I'm not at liberty to discuss this with you. Now, if you don't mind . . ."

I was being dismissed, but I hated to leave without knowing what was going on. Oz knew he was going to die; he'd told me as much. And he seemed okay with that. His only concern seemed to be finding the gold that would pay for his granddaughter's education. I realized that as much as I wanted to help Oz, the only thing I could do for him at that point was solve the riddle and find the treasure.

"'Life is love's legacy'?" Pappy said a short while later as I sat with him, Nick, Ethan, and Hazel at a long table in the library.

"I suppose it could mean he had a new life, or maybe since he was a doctor, he gave someone a new life," Hazel guessed.

"How are we supposed to use that to point us in the direction we need to go next to find the gold?" Ethan asked.

"And what about the legacy?" Hazel asked. "Was the life that was saved the legacy?"

"It has to be the masthead," I decided. "The masthead was carved as a legacy to the woman Warren Goldberg planned to marry. We already discussed the fact that it didn't make sense that he would display the symbol of his love for this woman in a bordello. What if Warren Goldberg wasn't the owner of the bar? What if he was the town's doctor? Maybe he came west to seek his fortune, or perhaps to heal his broken heart, bringing the masthead with him. When he arrived he saw that the town was really in need of a medic, so he sold the masthead to the bar owner to start the clinic."

"I thought the man started off as a ship owner," Pappy pointed out. "It doesn't make sense that he was a doctor."

"True," I admitted. "Maybe Warren Goldberg wasn't a doctor; maybe he donated the money to build the clinic. We have to try to figure out who owned what and take it from there."

"They didn't have records back then like we do now," Ethan said.

"I guess that means we're back to the letters and journals. There must be some mention of the names of the doctor and the man who owned the bar. And if Warren was neither of those men, we need to know where he fit in."

"Even a better question is where Oz's grandfather fit into all of this," Pappy added.

The next several hours were spent drinking coffee and reading letters and journals. It was interesting reading, but so far the activity hadn't moved us any closer to finding the gold.

"I think I found something," Nick spoke up after a while. He began to read aloud from the document he was holding.

"'Colt bought that hunk of wood Warren has been hauling around and set it up in the bar. I thought it was a bad idea and a waste of money, but Colt said it was for a good cause and the men seem to love it. I wouldn't be surprised if the bar is renamed The Maiden after all the attention she is getting.'"

"Okay, so someone named Colt owned the bar," I summarized. "Colt bought the maiden from Warren. We can assume that the money was used to fund the clinic. Question is, why did Warren sell his prized possession only to donate it to the clinic unless he was the doctor?"

"Maybe Oz's grandfather was the doctor," Nick speculated.

"No, Oz said his grandfather was a miner," Zoe corrected.

"Besides," Hazel stopped us, "we don't know that Warren used the money to fund the clinic. I admit it seems like a possibility based on the inscription on the seal, but we don't really know that for a fact."

Ethan pushed the book he was reading aside. "As interesting as this all is, I don't see how it helps us find the gold. What difference does it make whether Oz's grandfather was the doctor or not, or whether Warren sold the masthead to fund the clinic? Finding the answers to these questions won't bring us any closer to our goal."

"True," I acknowledged. "We have to be missing something."

"The riddle said something about hidden text," Pappy commented.

I read the note again:

To find what's next
You must reveal
The hidden text
In the medic's seal.

"Let's forget about who did what for a minute," Nick said. "Let's just look at the text on the seal."

"It says hidden text, but I didn't see any," I informed the group. "Maybe there were hidden words in the design."

"'Life is love's legacy,'" Hazel repeated. "It's beautiful. If this were one of my romances we'd find out that Warren carved the masthead as a legacy for his one true love, but in the end he sold his carving when he realized that love's true legacy is life."

I smiled as Hazel got a dreamy look on her face. She really was a romantic at heart.

"The fact that the clues were in the hidden compartment of the masthead and on the seal in the clinic is causing us to link the two," Ethan pointed out. "We don't know that Warren used the money to start the clinic; the letter just said he sold the masthead for a good cause. Maybe the words on the seal and the sale of the artifact have nothing at all to do with the gold. It could be that Oz's grandpa just knew about the hidden drawer and realized it would be a good hiding place for a clue."

"And the seal? Why choose that?" I asked.

"Maybe the guy was at the clinic due to an illness. He realized that he needed to hide his gold, so he got the idea to create a treasure hunt. He might have been sitting there, waiting for the doctor, looked at the wall, seen a message in the seal, and run with it."

"Yeah, but why a treasure hunt?" Pappy asked the question aloud that I had been asking myself all day. "If he wanted his son to have the gold why not just give it to him?"

"Maybe he wanted his son to have to work for his inheritance," Ethan suggested. "You did say the two didn't get along."

I frowned. "Hazel's interpretation is more romantic."

"You're trying to attribute a heartfelt motive to the man's actions when one may not exist," Ethan insisted. "The man lived his life in Devil's Den. He spent enough time in the saloon/bordello to know about the hidden drawer. So far, not one thing we know about this man makes it seem like he was a romantic at heart."

Ethan had a point, even though I wished he didn't. I'd let myself get caught up in the romance of the whole thing when we didn't even know where Oz's grandpa and the gold fit into the story. Maybe I needed to take another look at things without the blinders of romance coloring my perspective.

"Let's assume for a minute that the clinic and the masthead aren't associated with each other and Oz's grandfather simply chose the two locations for his clues due to nothing more than opportunity. What's the hidden message in the seal and how can it lead us to the gold?"

"Okay, so 'Life is love's legacy' meant something to the doctor, but let's assume it didn't have a specific meaning to Oz's grandfather," Pappy said. "Maybe the letters in the words mean something."

"What about the word on the bottom?" Nick asked. "LIV. Maybe that's the clue. It can be read literally as a word, but it could also stand for something."

"Like what?" I asked.

"I don't know. There are tons of acronyms out there. Maybe LIV is an acronym for a phrase that was popular at the time the seal was developed."

"Or maybe, like the text, it has a Latin interpretation," Hazel suggested.

"Or a Roman one," I realized. "LIV is the Roman numeral for 54, and I just saw that in one of these books."

I pulled the books I had most recently sifted through toward me and began thumbing through them. "I remember there was a newspaper article with the number 54 in the headline. It seems like it was from the *Chronicle*. It wasn't in the photo album; maybe it was in the journal we were reading." I opened the book and leafed through. "Here it is." I pointed to the yellowed paper someone had glued into the journal. "This article is titled A TRIBUTE TO THE 54. The article *is* from the *Chronicle*, and it's dated October 12, 1910. There's a photo of a bunch of men and a couple of women standing in front of the clinic. The article states:

"A year ago today fifty-four men from the small mining camp of Devil's Den pooled their meager resources to bring a doctor from our local hospital to their small village to save the life of a prostitute who had developed complications from a late-term pregnancy. Dr. Owen Ozwald, a recently hired resident at the hospital, was chosen for the task. Upon his arrival at the camp, the doctor found admiration and affection for a community that had come together to save the life of one of their own. Dr. Ozwald was so moved by the commitment of the community to save a single life that he handed in his resignation and announced plans to move his family to Devil's Den in order to open a clinic for those who live in the area. The highly anticipated Devil's Den Medical Clinic opened today and the entire town came out for the celebration. Lilly England, the local madame, who acts as a mother of sorts to the girls, attributes the close-knit community and the willingness of its members to make sacrifices for one another with its isolation from the outside world."

"So Oz's grandfather *was* the doctor," Hazel concluded.

"I thought you said Oz told you he never knew his grandfather because he abandoned his family to chase the gold rush when his father was a small boy,"

Pappy said. "It doesn't sound like that's what happened at all."

"Maybe that's just what Oz's grandmother told Oz's father. I suppose she might not have wanted to make the move and opted to stay behind."

"I guess when you marry a doctor you have a certain expectation as to the lifestyle you'll live," Hazel commented.

"So what now?" I asked. "As interesting as this is, I don't see how it helps us find the gold."

"Look at the photo," Pappy said. "The doctor has his arm around the woman on his right. Based on the way she's dressed, I'd be willing to bet she's Lilly England, and the woman on the left with the baby is the prostitute he must have saved. Maybe Oz's grandfather and this Lilly were friends. Maybe we can find a clue by taking a closer look at her."

"Why would they be friends?" I asked.

"They both seemed to care about people," Nick pointed out. "Dr. Ozwald so much so that he gave up his affluent lifestyle to move to the camp, and Lilly took in strays and gave them jobs."

"She made them hookers," Hazel clarified.

"Yes, she made them hookers," Nick agreed. "But maybe Oz's grandpa saw beyond the questionable occupation of the local women and developed a true affection for them."

"It does seem like there's a certain intimacy in the way they're leaning into one another," Hazel admitted.

"Okay, say that's true. So what?" I sighed. "How does that help us find the gold?"

"Maybe Dr. Ozwald gave the gold to Lilly for safekeeping," Nick suggested.

"That's a long shot," I responded, "and even if he did, how's that going to help us? Lilly is long dead."

For the first time I realized that this treasure hunt might not have a satisfactory ending.

"The house that Lilly and the girls lived in is still standing. Why don't we go have a look?" Nick said.

We all looked at one another and shrugged. I doubted we'd find anything, but it certainly couldn't hurt. It seemed a shame to give up when we had come so far, and we didn't have any other theories. Even Hazel did something she never does; she closed the library so she could come along with us. It was an adventure we all wanted to be around for the conclusion of.

I called the hospital and spoke to Dr. Westlake. He told me Oz was still alive, but his prognosis had been downgraded. Dr. Westlake wanted to move him to a larger facility in the valley, but Oz had refused to go. I asked if his granddaughter had been notified and he promised to look into it.

"You know what's occurred to me," I said as we walked toward Pappy's Suburban, the only vehicle large enough to hold all of us. "If Dr. Ozwald truly wanted his son to have the gold why did he make it so hard?"

"If the son had come to Devil's Den in 1940, as I assume Dr. Ozwald thought he would, Lilly and the other town folk would have been alive to welcome him and, I assume, lead him to his inheritance," Pappy answered. "My guess is that Dr. Ozwald simply wanted to provide an intriguing enough situation so that the son would come to the town he obviously loved."

"But he never did," I said. "It's really kind of sad. It sounds like Dr. Ozwald moved to Devil's Den when Oz's father was fairly young. I doubt we'll ever know why he made the choice to leave his family behind, but I do get the feeling that the man wasn't the monster Oz and his dad had been led to believe."

The house Lilly and her girls had lived in was on the outskirts of town, a large two-story structure in an advanced state of disrepair. It had been abandoned ever since I'd been alive, and I wouldn't be surprised to learn that it hadn't been lived in since Lilly herself had passed away. The drive to the house wasn't paved and the dirt drive hadn't been graded, so after countless winters of runoff the ride to the structure was bumpy at best.

"So what are we looking for?" Hazel asked Pappy as he pulled up to the front of the house.

"I don't really know. I guess I just hope that if there's something to find we'll recognize it when we see it."

Pappy took Hazel's arm and cautioned the rest of us to tread gently as we made our way up the rotted steps to the equally rotted front porch. The door was unlocked, yet it took both Pappy and Nick to push it open after years of nonuse. The house was covered in dust and cobwebs, and I was certain I heard scurrying on the hardwood floors as we walked into the entry. I had to suppress a shudder as the similarities to Hezekiah Henderson's house flashed through my mind. Like the Henderson house, it seemed most of the furnishings that had been in place when Lilly was alive still remained.

"I suggest we split up," Ethan said. "Zoe and I can take the upstairs and the three of you take the downstairs. Holler if you find anything."

Ethan and I were the two youngest members of the group, so it made sense that we should tackle the rickety stairs, but I still wished I'd been chosen to stay on the lower level, where the odds of falling through the floor were much lower.

The second story of the house was made up of small bedrooms that I assumed had been assigned to Lilly's girls. I was surprised to find them furnished tastefully. They would have fit well in any house in America at that time. I don't know what I was expecting. Mirrors on the ceilings? Chains hanging from the walls? At the end of the hall was a larger room, which I assumed belonged to Lilly.

"It looks like these stairs go to the attic," Ethan informed me as we came to a crossroads. "I'll look up there and you check out the bedroom."

I was glad Ethan had suggested that Charlie and I take the bedroom and not the attic. I couldn't quite shake the feeling that creatures were waiting to jump out at me.

The bedroom was large and filled with natural sunlight. As in the other rooms, it looked as if much of the furniture that had been in the house when Lilly lived there remained. I began to open drawers and sort through the contents in the hope of finding something that would tell us why Oz's grandfather had sent us here, if he had in fact even intended Lilly's home to be part of the treasure hunt.

I couldn't imagine how everything we'd learned during this journey fit together. Maybe, as Ethan had speculated, it didn't. Maybe the clues were random, chosen due to nothing more than opportunity, but somehow I felt like the steps we'd taken had been carefully orchestrated with a clearly defined motive in mind.

I was sorting through the item in the nightstand when Charlie began scratching at the floor in the corner of the room. I found myself cringing. Most of the time when Charlie scratched at an enclosed space there was a body on the other side. I made my way to the spot where he was standing atop a large throw rug.

"Whatcha got?" I asked.

Charlie barked once and then returned to his digging motion. I pulled back the rug, and sure enough, there was a trapdoor that appeared to be latched but not locked. I slid back the latch and opened the wooden panel. Inside the small space was a box that also was latched but unlocked. I opened the box and found a smaller box, which contained letters bound together with a yellowed string. Beneath the letters was a leather pouch I hoped would be the gold we'd been looking for.

"Find anything?" Ethan walked up behind me. I slipped the letters into my jacket and handed him the pouch. He opened it and looked inside. "Well, I'll be."

Chapter 3

I wasn't able to get in to see Oz until the next day. I called early that morning and was told that if I showed up at eleven o'clock I could probably have a short visit. I was excited not only to tell Oz that we'd found the gold but that I'd found the answers to questions he most likely never even knew he had.

I'd read some of the letters Lilly had tucked away. Many of them had been written to the son of the doctor that had been mailed but returned unopened. It seemed that Oz's grandfather had not had a happy marriage even before he'd moved to Devil's Den. His wife had married him for the prestige that came from being a doctor's wife and just as quickly dumped him when he decided to follow his heart. Eventually, Lilly and Dr. Ozwald made a life together. They never had children of their own, though it seemed they'd cared deeply for the girls they took under their wings. While many of the women continued to dance at the local bar, once Dr. Oz came onto the scene most of the women retired from other more physically intimate means of earning money.

I believe Dr. Oz created the treasure hunt in the hope that his son would come to Devil's Den and learn the truth of what had occurred, but he never did. I was happy to tell Oz that his grandfather not only had chosen the same nickname he had but was a kind man with a good heart who hadn't abandoned his family in the pursuit of gold but simply followed his heart where it led.

"I'm here to visit Mr. Ozwald," I informed the woman at the desk.

"I have instructions for you to speak to Dr. Westlake when you get here. He's in his office. You can go on in."

I had a bad feeling about this, but I headed toward the office as directed. I knew before Dr. Westlake said anything that Oz would not be present for the final chapter in the story of his life.

"Zoe, please come in. Have a seat."

"Oz?" I asked, remaining standing.

"I'm afraid he passed this morning."

I felt myself tear up.

"He went peacefully in his sleep."

"And his granddaughter?" I choked.

"She arrived shortly after he passed. I called to speak to her this morning. She's staying at the Serenity Motor Inn. I figured you'd want to talk to her, and she's agreed to meet you at Rosie's at noon. Did you find what you were looking for?"

"Actually, I did."

I stood outside the now vacant room Oz had occupied and said my good-byes, then took the gold and the letters I'd found and headed to Rosie's. I rehearsed the tale I was going to share with the granddaughter Oz had loved so much. I'd tell her how much he had loved her, and that his final wish had been that she use the gold to pursue her dream. I'd tell her that in the short time I'd known this extraordinary man, he'd changed my perspective on many things. I'd share how the quest on which he'd sent me had opened my eyes to a world I'd never realized existed. I'd look her in the eye and tell her how this voyage had left me with a new sense of pride in the town where I was born, and I'd share with her how this exceptional man and his final request had touched my life in a way I'd never forget.

I thought about the men and women in the photographs. I felt like I'd had an opportunity to peek into their lives. Winter was about to descend upon us, but I knew in the spring Charlie and I would hike up the mountain and plant some flowers to honor the brave men and women who first made their lives in the warm embrace of the rugged mountains I now call home.

Recipes From Rosie's Kitchen

Timberland Shrimp Chowder
Cheesy Chicken Chowder
Mountain Man Beef Stew
Italian Beef Sandwiches
Pizza Rolls
Ramen and Noodles
Pot Roast with Sour Cream Sauce
Pumpkin Patch Muffins
Ellie's Pumpkin Cheesecake
Pumpkin Cookies
Apple Cranberry Crisp
Halloween Snack Mix

Timberland Shrimp Chowder

Base:
1 cube butter
½ chopped onion (or more if you like onion)
3-4 cloves garlic chopped
6 cups of peeled and diced potato (frozen hash browns work as well)
2 pounds cooked shrimp (any size, Rosie uses medium but she has used salad shrimp in a pinch.)
32 oz chicken broth (can use part chicken broth and part water if preferred)

Spices: amounts can be adjusted to accommodate taste.
¼ tsp chili powder
¼ tsp cayenne pepper
¼ tsp ground cumin
¼ tsp coriander
½ tsp nutmeg
½ tsp paprika
1 tsp salt
1 tsp white pepper

Melt butter in heavy pan
Sauté onion and garlic
Add potatoes and shrimp
Cover with chicken broth (just enough to boil potatoes)
Add spices
Boil until potatoes are tender – this time will vary depending on the size of potato cubes

Cheese Sauce: While potatoes are boiling use a separate pan to make cheese sauce
1 cube butter
4 oz cream cheese (1 small or ½ large package)
1 cup heavy cream
2 cups shredded cheddar cheese (do not use non or low fat)
2 cups grated parmesan cheese (or 1 cup parmesan and 1 cup romano)

Melt butter in pan over med heat. Add cream cheese. Stir until melted. Add cream. Add cheese a little at a time.

After potatoes are tender slowly fold cheese sauce into base. Stir constantly until well blended.

Cheesy Chicken Chowder

3 cups chicken broth
2 cups diced potatoes
1 cup diced carrots
1 cup diced celery
½ cup diced onion
Salt
Pepper
¼ cup butter
1/3 cup flour
2 cups heavy cream
2 cups shredded cheddar
2 cups cooked and cubed chicken

Bring chicken broth to a boil. Reduce heat. Add potatoes, carrots, celery, salt and pepper. Cover and simmer until vegetables are tender.

Meanwhile melt butter in saucepan. Add flour and mix well. Gradually stir in cream. Cook over low heat until slightly thickened. Stir in cheese. Heat until melted. Add broth along with chicken. Cook over low heat until warmed through.

Mountain Man Beef Stew

2 pounds boneless chuck cut into cubes (or precut stew meat)
2 Tbs veg oil
3 large baking potatoes cut into cubes
1 large onion peeled and chopped
4 large carrots cut into bite size pieces
1 cup sliced mushrooms
1 can artichoke hearts – quartered
3 Tbs flour
1 cup beef broth
1 cup burgundy wine (Or other red)
3 bay leaves
1 tsp basil
Seasoned salt, garlic powder, and pepper

Season meat with salt, garlic powder, and pepper and then brown beef in hot vegetable oil. Add all the vegetables except mushrooms and artichoke hearts. Sauté over medium heat for about 5 minutes. Sprinkle flour over meat and vegetables and stir to coat. Add broth, wine, bay leaves and basil. Bring to a boil and then cover and lower heat. Simmer for about 1 ½ hours until vegetables are tender. Add mushrooms and artichokes during last half hour.

Italian Beef Sandwiches

1 boneless chuck roast (3-4 pounds) trimmed of fat
and cut in half
3 TBS dried basil
3 TBS dried oregano
1 cup water
1 envelope onion soup mix
I cup Mozzarella grated
Italian Rolls (or other rolls)

Place roast in slow cooker. Add water and spices.
Pour soup over top. Cover and cook 7-8 hours.
Shred meat spoon onto Italian rolls
Sprinkle Mozzarella over the top
Broil until cheese is golden

Pizza Rolls

1 loaf frozen bread thawed
½ cup grated Mozzarella Cheese
½ cup grated Cheddar Cheese
½ cup grated Parmesan Cheese/
4 ounces pepperoni (or other pizza topping)
3 TBS butter –melted

Roll a loaf of the bread so that it is flat
Place Mozzarella Cheese, Cheddar Cheese, and pepperoni in center
Fold in both ends of loaf and then roll so that seam is on the bottom.
Slice rolls into 12 pieces and place in greased 9X13 baking pan
Brush butter over the top of each roll
Sprinkle with Parmesan Cheese
Let rise until double in size
Bake at 375 degrees for 15 – 20 minutes

(Zoe often uses extra cheese and sliced black olives)
Serve with ranch or bleu cheese dressing for dipping

Ramen and Noodles

1 pound of ground beef
2 packages of Ramen Noodles (beef) – crunched up
2 ½ cup water
I can oriental vegetables - drained
¼ tsp ginger

In a large skillet brown ground beef. Add contents of one of the flavoring packets. Remove meat.

In same skillet combine water, vegetables, ginger, noodles, and contents of remaining flavor packet.

Bring to a boil. Reduce heat. Cover and simmer 3-4 minutes

Return beef to the pan. Cook 2-3 minutes.

Serve with rice.

Pot Roast with Sour Cream Sauce

1 boneless beef chuck roast (appox. 3 pounds)
2 cups baby carrots
4 cups washed and cubed potatoes
1 cup of mushrooms – cleaned and sliced
1 jar (5oz) horseradish well drained
1 envelope onion soup mix
1 can golden mushroom soup
1 cup sour cream

Place vegetables in slow cooker
Rub beef with horseradish and place over vegetables
Sprinkle with onion soup
Pour -mushroom soup over top cook 8-10 hours (until meat is done – cooking time will vary greatly depending on slow cooker used)

Remove beef and veggies – stir sour cream into juices with a wire whisk
Pour gravy over meat and veggies and enjoy

Pumpkin Patch Muffins

3 cups sugar
1 cup vegetable oil
4 eggs
1 16 oz can pumpkin (2 cups)
½ cup water
3 ½ cups flour
2 tsp baking soda
1 tsp baking powder
½ tsp salt
1 Tbs cinnamon
1 tsp ginger
1 tsp ground nutmeg
½ tsp ground nutmeg
½ tsp ground cloves
½ tsp all spice
4 cups walnuts "Chopped)

Combine: sugar, oil, and eggs. Add pumpkin and water and mix well.
Combine dry ingredients and add to pumpkin mixture.
Add nuts.

Spoon into greased cupcake pans (or use papers)
Bake at 350 degrees for 28 – 30 minutes

Cream Cheese Frosting (optional)
¾ cup of butter softened
6 oz cream cheese softened
1 tsp vanilla
3 cups powdered sugar

Whip all ingredients together – spread onto cooled
muffins

Ellie's Pumpkin Cheesecake

1 box of graham cracker crust – follow directions on box to make 9x13 pan
4 packages cream cheese – softened
1 ½ cups sugar
16 oz pumpkin
¾ cup whipping cream
3 Tbs flour
½ tsp nutmeg
½ tsp ginger
½ tsp cinnamon
½ tsp ground cloves
¼ tsp salt
¼ tsp vanilla
6 eggs

Beat together cream cheese and sugar. Add pumpkin, whipping cream, flour, spices, and vanilla. Mix. Add 4 whole eggs plus 2 egg yolks.

Pour over prepared graham cracker crust.
Bake at 325 until toothpick comes out clean – about an hour
Refrigerate

Topping:
½ cup sugar
2 cups whipping cream
½ cup powdered sugar
¼ tsp vanilla

Whip until fluffy. Spread over chilled cheesecake.

Pumpkin Cookies

½ cup margarine
3 cups sugar
1 can pumpkin (15 oz)
2 eggs
½ cup milk
6 cups flour
2 tsp baking soda
2 tsp cinnamon
1 tsp salt
1 tsp allspice
½ tsp ground cloves
1 cup finely chopped walnuts

In a large mixing bowl cream the shortening and the sugar.
Beat in Pumpkins, eggs, and milk
Add dry ingredients and mix thoroughly
Add nuts
Drop onto greased baking sheet
Bake at 375 degrees for approx. 12 minutes or until lightly browned
Cool completely and then frost

Frosting – mix all ingredients below together until smooth
¾ Cup butter softened
6 oz cream cheese softened
1 TBS vanilla
3 Cups Powdered sugar
1 tsp cinnamon

Rosie's Apple Crisp

4 cups of apples peeled, cored, and sliced thin
1 cup cranberries
½ cup sugar
2 Tbs cinnamon
2 tsp ground nutmeg
½ cup quick cooking oats
½ cup flour
½ cup brown sugar
½ cup butter cut into pieces
1 cup chopped pecan
1 jar caramel sauce (the kind used for ice cream is fine)

In a large bowl mix apples, cranberries, white sugar, cinnamon, and nutmeg. Place in buttered 9x13 baking dish.

Combine oats, flour, and brown sugar. With a fork mix butter in until crumbly.
Stir in pecans. Spread over apples. Drizzle with caramel sauce.
Bake in preheated oven at 375 degrees for 40 to 50 minutes or until apples are tender.

Serve with vanilla ice cream

Halloween Snack Mix

6 cups caramel corn
2 cups salted cashews
2 cups candy corn
½ cup dried cranberries
Large bag of Halloween M&M's

Mix together and store in airtight container

Author Bio

Kathi Daley lives with her husband, kids, grandkids, and Bernese mountain dogs in beautiful Lake Tahoe. When she isn't writing, she likes to read (preferably at the beach or by the fire), cook (preferably something with chocolate or cheese), and garden (planting and planning, not weeding). She also enjoys spending time on the water when she's not hiking, biking, or snowshoeing the miles of desolate trails surrounding her home.

Kathi uses the mountain setting in which she lives, along with the animals (wild and domestic) that share her home, as inspiration for her cozy mysteries.

Stay up to date with her newsletter, *The Daley Weekly*. There's a link to sign up on both her Facebook page and her website, or you can access the sign-in sheet at: http://eepurl.com/NRPDf

Visit Kathi:
Facebook at Kathi Daley Books,
www.facebook.com/kathidaleybooks
Twitter at Kathi Daley@kathidaley
Webpage www.kathidaley.com
E-mail kathidaley@kathidaley.com

88827071R00121

Made in the USA
Middletown, DE
12 September 2018